Last Stop, Wylder

by

Barbara Bettis

The Wylder West Series

Last Stop, Wylder

Cover Art by *The Wild Rose Press, Inc.*

The Wild Rose Press, Inc.
PO Box 708
Adams Basin, NY 14410-0708
Visit us at www.thewildrosepress.com

Publishing History
First Edition, 2022
Trade Paperback ISBN 978-1-5092-4348-8
Digital ISBN 978-1-5092-4349-5

The Wylder West Series
Published in the United States of America

Emily stood outside the station in Cheyenne, waiting to board the smaller train that would take her the final fifteen miles east to Wylder. A single passenger carriage brought up the end of four freight cars on the short spur line.

The breeze here was cooler than the hot, dry gusts at her last stop in Nebraska. Her dark blue traveling suit felt rather comfortable for once.

She moved closer to the train. *Wouldn't do to miss the conductor's call.* Noise swirled around like the notes of a discordant band, and she might miss the announcement. Quite a din, with cattle complaining and stomping, teams of horses blowing and snorting, harness and reins jangling, wagons creaking and wheels squeaking, laughter and cursing. Not once did a woman's voice ride the shoulder of a shout.

Farther up the track, a man in a red shirt led a horse as it clopped up a wooden ramp into one of the stock units. Several head of cattle had already been locked into a different car. Looked like more livestock than people traveled to Wylder.

The breeze carried another sharp smell of cattle…she sneezed…and dust. Occasionally an odor of rancid hot grease puffed by from a small restaurant just down from the depot. She paced a few steps up then back. Not long now before she reached David and the next chapter of her life.

Ahead, the man reappeared and leaped to the ground from the stock car, his movements smooth, graceful. He swooped up a saddle and swung it onto his left shoulder.

All in one movement. How did he do that? She couldn't look away.

Praise for Barbara Bettis

Dedication

From the bottom of my heart, I thank these fabulous ladies:
My wonderful on-line critique group, Ana, Karen, Dawn, Ruth, Tess, and Lane; Kathleen, for her valuable insight, keen eye, and kind encouragement; my fabulous editor, Nicole; and to my morning writing buddies, Lisa and Claudia--I couldn't have finished this without all of you!

Chapter 1

Colorado Territory
July, 1878

From the crest of a bluff east of Denver, Morgan Dodd considered his future.

A new start where no one knew his name. A new life.

West to California? Beyond the snow-flecked mountains to his left, barely visible in the early evening haze. A land of opportunity with booming cities and wide valleys to ranch.

He shifted in the saddle, his gaze drifting northwest. Oregon, maybe. Word of rich, fertile land sounded mighty appealing. He could settle down there, farm a little. If he remembered how to farm. God knew, it'd been long enough.

First, though, north to Cheyenne. Where one last job awaited—and the money for that new start, wherever it lay.

Morgan glanced again at the blue-shrouded foothills to his left. The unknown. Deep in his chest, a hitch of anticipation had him straightening. If he rode hard, he could reach Denver by dark. Then at first light, off to start over. Perhaps…

Something moved. His attention focused on the edge of a clearing below. In the wan light, three antelope ventured from a clot of trees to sample the tall, lush grass of mid July, tender again after last night's rain.

His brief reflections forgotten, Morgan brought up his Winchester and sighted. For a moment he hesitated. The three animals were beautiful. Young, their lives ahead of them. He hated for a gun to change one forever. Nostalgia hit him, as unexpected as it was unwelcome. He swallowed it.

He had a duty, and he'd best get it done. One shot brought down the biggest of the trio, sending the other two leaping for cover.

A breeze carried the distant murmur of cattle settling in for the night on rich grazing ground to the east. Morgan dismounted and strode to collect his kill. Tomorrow his fellows on the drive would dine on something other than beans and rabbit.

Then they'd head out for the rail head in Cheyenne. *Cheyenne.*

His path had always been set. A new job. Gunhand for a Union Pacific agent.

He threw one last glance toward the mountains.

Maybe next year.

****

Union Pacific Station
Omaha, Neb.
July, 1878

Emily Martin waved from the lowered window of the train car outside the Omaha Depot for the Union Pacific Railroad.

"Goodbye, Mama, Papa," she mouthed over the noise of the idling engine. A puff of sooty smoke curled in, and she coughed then struggled to raise the glass.

2

Her action smothered her parents' words, but she knew them by rote. *Be careful. Write often. I wish you would reconsider. I'll transfer you money.*

Her mother dabbed a linen handkerchief at the corners of her eyes. Her father slid his arm around his wife's shoulders. Bless their protective hearts, they'd come all the way to Omaha with her to see her off on her journey.

Only the fact that she was able to secure a sleeping car had made them agree not to accompany her to Wyoming. That and the fact one of her father's fellow attorneys, Mr. Hamilton, and his wife were on the same train enroute to San Francisco to visit their son. The Hamiltons had promised to look out for Emily.

But for all intents, she was alone.

She pressed a hand against her chest—as if that could stop her heart jumping.

On her own for the first time in all her twenty-two years.

Even at Stephens College she'd been surrounded by other girls like herself. But now she headed into the unknown, to Wylder, Wyoming, for a long visit with her brother.

At the engine's shrill whistle, her mother jumped and pressed closer to her father. The train gave an impatient lurch, like a dog straining at the leash. Her heart echoed the movement. As the car jerked into motion, she waved one last time. Then she leaned back.

And sighed.

Chapter 2

Emily stood outside the station in Cheyenne, waiting to board the smaller train that would take her the final fifteen miles east to Wylder. A single passenger carriage brought up the end of four freight cars on the short spur line.

The breeze here was cooler than the hot, dry gusts at her last stop in Nebraska. Her dark blue traveling suit felt rather comfortable for once.

She moved closer to the train. *Wouldn't do to miss the conductor's call.* Noise swirled around like the notes of a discordant band, and she might miss the announcement. Quite a din, with cattle complaining and stomping, teams of horses blowing and snorting, harness and reins jangling, wagons creaking and wheels squeaking, laughter and cursing. Not once did a woman's voice ride the shoulder of a shout.

Farther up the track, a man in a red shirt led a horse as it clopped up a wooden ramp into one of the stock units. Several head of cattle had already been locked into a different car. Looked like more livestock than people traveled to Wylder.

The breeze carried another sharp smell of cattle…she sneezed…and dust. Occasionally an odor of rancid hot grease puffed by from a small restaurant just down from the depot. She paced a few steps up then back. Not long now before she reached David and the next chapter of her life.

Ahead, the man reappeared and leaped to the ground from the stock car, his movements smooth, graceful. He swooped up a saddle and swung it onto his left shoulder.

All in one movement. How did he do that? She couldn't look away. Tall, lean, dark-haired, anchoring the saddle with one hand, dangling a grayish-brown hat in the other, he ambled toward her.

His strides were fluid but sure, mesmerizing. She caught her breath. Like a prowl. Like...yes, he moved like the puma she saw at the Chicago Zoo last year. Confident yet wary, relaxed but watchful, easy but relentless.

Her stomach tilted at his lanky grace, the way his broad shoulders carried the saddle yet managed to hold straight, even a little jaunty—challenging. A shiver shot up her spine and she looked away. *Goodness. I hope he didn't notice me staring.*

She'd never seen someone move like that. Perhaps the contained, almost challenging, gait was typical of Western men. But none of the scores of other men she'd glimpsed during the journey had that kind of presence.

His red shirt, calico she saw now, looked clean but wrinkled, as if it had been wadded in the bottom of a bag.

"Excuse me, miss." The conductor stood in the doorway of the passenger car. "You can board now." He jumped down the steps to hand her up, as politely as if they were still in the City.

"Thank you." Emily smiled, grasped his fingers, and lifted the hem of her skirt. Inside, she considered the empty seats, then chose one three rows down the aisle next to the window so she would have a good view of the scenery.

From behind her rose the murmurs of two men, then came a thud. She started and glanced over her shoulder. The man in red had dropped his saddle to the floor and was seating himself in the back row on the opposite side of the aisle.

He looked up and caught her eye. His head drooped in a slight nod, and he placed his hat on the seat adjoining his. Her chin ducked in a minute response before she whipped her gaze to the front. And pressed a hand against her suddenly thudding heart. She inhaled deeply and eased out a long, silent sigh. *No need to be nervous.* This was friendly behavior and absolutely normal for the informal Westerners. *At least that's what David claimed in his letters.*

A few other passengers boarded, and the chatter of voices grew louder. All male. These past days of travel she'd grown used to being one of few, if not the lone, female around. She saw only their backs as they trooped by and found seats farther to the front. Two were dressed in suits, but three were outfitted like the man in red, with dark trousers and cotton shirts. Except those three hadn't bothered to bathe or change their clothing lately.

Emily had grown up around men. Politicians, businessmen, and other professionals frequently visited at her family's home. An influential attorney, her father moved in many circles. And her personal, political, and writing interests led her to male-dominated meetings. So she was used to being around members of the opposite sex of all ages.

She'd never been around so many unfamiliar men alone, however. Men whose ways of life were unlike any she'd experienced.

Making a concentrated effort to regulate her breathing, she stared out the window. Cheyenne bustled with activity—men in suits, and men in trousers and shirts and vests, men in waist overalls. Several of those wore the new-style hat David had described. It had a wider brim and a taller, straight-sided crown. What had he called it—Boss of the West? He'd said many of the cowboys wore such headgear. But where were all the women? Surely a lot lived in a town this size.

That's right. Today's Sunday. Perhaps they were at church, or home preparing lunch. But Emily found it odd that so many businesses remained open on Sunday out here.

Behind her, a slight commotion signaled another arrival. The newcomer strode down the aisle, greeting the others as he approached. They rose to shake his hand.

"Foster," said one of the men. "Didn't know you were back from the East. How was business?"

"Damned fine," answered a loud, commanding voice. When the other man cleared his throat and glanced toward Emily, the speaker turned. In the instant before he spoke again, his gaze raked her. She lifted her chin and smoothed her features. It was an automatic reaction she'd learned over the past few years. The politic response to an encroaching man's expression.

The speaker strode the few steps to her. He doffed his hat, a black bowler. "Beg pardon, ma'am. Didn't realize a lady was present." He held out his hand. Automatically she placed her gloved fingertips on his, and he bowed. Smooth as any greeting she'd receive at a social gathering at home. She dipped her head in his direction and reclaimed her hand.

"Out this way, we don't have the luxury of third party introductions." His tone was smooth, friendly.

Too friendly. A chill skittered down her back.

"So allow me," he continued. "I'm Eli Foster, Wylder's representative of our host, here, the Union Pacific. I assume you're traveling to Wylder. Only place to be going on this line." His chuckle sounded *pro forma*—smooth, deprecating, condescending.

He modeled the gracious, avuncular man-of-substance greeting reserved for ladies. But his eyes still sized her up. Her chin rose again while her spine stiffened.

"Wylder's a fine, growing place. Allow me to welcome you," he said. "Are you visiting relatives there, Miss…?"

"Thank you for the kind greeting, Mr. Foster," she said in her best meeting-strangers-during-a-reception tone. "I look forward to seeing the town."

Before he could further press for her name, a shrill whistle pierced the air, and the train lurched forward, causing him to stumble backward. He straightened and repositioned his hat.

"I'd best get to my seat and find my ticket before our conductor scolds me. Hope to see you in Wylder, ma'am." Foster turned and made his way back to the other men, steadying his gait by clutching the backs of seats along the aisle.

Well. Emily had received her first welcome to her new home. She supposed he appeared to be a pleasant, mannerly gentleman. In his late thirties, perhaps, he was handsome enough. Yet something about the Union Pacific representative made her uncomfortable, in addition to the way he'd looked her over. His smooth words and too-confident behavior sent prickles across her shoulders. Rather like some politicians she'd met.

No, no! No more politics. She'd promised herself that when she left Kansas City. David wanted help with the paper he'd taken over, and a growing Western town was just what she needed. New and different surroundings. Peace and quiet and the homey news of a small place. Friends and neighbors, not critical politicians and competitive socialites.

Acceptance, not stilted courtesy and hastily hidden titters at an engagement broken simply because she authored a newspaper column now and then.

She settled back and pulled a book from her bag, Mark Twain's *The Gilded Age*. She had enjoyed Twain's short story about the jumping frog and looked forward to his novel.

She'd barely begun the story when a shadow fell across her vision.

"Excuse me, ma'am. You dropped this."

The warm, slightly rough voice sent an entirely different sort of shiver down her spine.

She looked up. Into gray eyes. Smoke eyes. *No one has smoke eyes, silly.* The self-scolding sent her gaze in a quick sweep of his face. Her breath clogged somewhere along her throat when she reached his mouth. Generous, wide, but not thick. One side of that wide, generous mouth was quirked up in a questioning way.

Oh. He'd said something she'd missed.

He lifted his hand, and her gaze flashed to a small

black diary with a tiny pencil attached by a blue ribbon. *Oh my.* The record of her thoughts during the journey. It must have fallen out when she retrieved her book.

She took it from his fingers—long, callused, tanned brown. On the side of his thumb a scar meandered, disappearing beneath his red shirt cuff like a thin white thread.

"Thank you." Years of training paid off—her voice remained steady. But her oddly dry mouth gave the words a touch of breathiness. Definitely unlike her.

Her gaze flicked over his face again, committing it to memory. A handy talent for a writer, one she'd had from childhood.

"You're welcome."

Chill bumps rose on her skin at the dark, rich tone of his voice. Morning chocolate flowing over shards of sugar. Oh good heavens, she was behaving like a silly ninny who'd never seen a man before.

The corner of his mouth raised in a polite smile, and he disappeared from her side. She followed the tap of his boots, the rustle of his sitting.

She absently slipped the notebook into her reticule bag and opened Mr. Twain. For the next several minutes, she stared at the book, seeing not the printed words, but the image of the cowboy, prowling across the page. Lean cheeks, square chin, dark brown hair curling along his neck, gray eyes piercing her from beneath long, thick black lashes, and eyebrows with a natural arch most women only dreamed of having.

His nose—long, narrow but strong. How could a nose be narrow and strong? She nearly turned for another look but stopped in time. *Great Aunt Maude! What am I doing?* Determined to banish the stranger from her mind, she watched the passing countryside as they traveled east and slightly south.

Occasional fields of grass dotted with grazing cattle interspersed with patches of strange rock formations. If she leaned close enough to the window, she caught glimpses of hills toward the side. A ridge of dark against the blue horizon gradually became the forms of…mountains.

She inhaled in wonder and took in dirt particles gusted from the wind outside combined with the movement of the train. Another firm puff of breeze brought smoke from the engine. The soot set off a round of coughing. While she dug in her reticule for her handkerchief, a dark form loomed at the side of her vision. The movement came so quickly, she instinctively ducked.

Instead of making impact, the figure—red, she saw—reached over her head to raise the window. A two-or-so inch crack remained open for air to circulate. The splash of red pulled back to resolve again into the cowboy from the back row.

"Now. Air enough for relief but without the dangers," he said, his low voice rippling along her nerves. Breathless, Emily gazed into his eyes through the blur of smoke-triggered tears. After another cough, she managed, "Thank you."

That half smile tugged his mouth again as he nodded. "Ma'am."

She blinked away the moisture and returned a tiny smile while she took in retreating wide shoulders, narrow hips, long legs. Her smile grew when she noticed the hat-edge indentation in his dark hair. A funny sliver of warmth lodged in her chest at the ordinary sign. Turning quickly, she stared out the window again.

There is nothing fascinating about that stranger.

She lifted the book and pretended to read.

The remainder of the journey proved unremarkable. Words of the businessmen at the front of the car, sounds of the three cowboys immersed in a game of cards, all nothing but murmurs beneath the clack of wheels against tracks. The sounds combined into a rhythm that lulled Emily into a semi-sleep until a squalling whistle and a sharp jerk threw her head against the window. A loud, sucking whoosh was followed by a clatter of a closing door.

"Wylder," the conductor yelled, striding along the aisle. "Last stop." He paused in front of her. "We're here, ma'am. I'll get one of the boys from the livery to haul your trunks. You just tell him where you're bound for."

"Thank you. You've been very helpful."

He rushed ahead to prepare for the passengers to unload.

She remained seated, preferring to wait for the others to pass. However, courtesy prevailed, and the men paused for her to go first. Smiling, she rose, collected her bag, and made her way to the back of the car. The man in red still sat, his attention on something outside the window.

The conductor handed her down the last huge step to ground packed by years of footsteps. "If you'll stand over there, ma'am, I'll see to your baggage."

"Over there" was a stretch of bare ground several feet from the depot. A streak of wind whipped around the building, tugging her hat and swirling dust into her eyes and nose. She turned away from the gust toward the train as she fumbled for her handkerchief. She coughed, then sneezed before she could pull it from her reticule.

She'd dabbed the moisture from her eyes when a flash of red caught her attention. The man from the back row stepped down, saddle on his left shoulder. His right hand swung free, brushing a gun holstered on his right hip.

Emily's heart jumped. Why had he strapped on a gun belt? None of the other men wore one, not that she'd noticed. Her gaze sped to the other cowboys who'd left the train, jostling each other as they neared the station. No firearms.

The man strode away, his gait smooth, easy, alert as he approached the car where his horse waited. She lost sight of him when a buckboard came rolling to a stop not far from her trunk and bags.

A youth leaped down, his freckled face beaming with a smile. "Ralph said I was to pick up a lady passenger. Reckon that's you, ma'am."

He loaded her baggage, then beckoned. "I'm Tommy. Just tell me where you want to go, and I'll see you get there."

He climbed onto the plank seat and waited while she walked to the buckboard. She'd never ridden in a vehicle quite like this, and she wasn't sure how to get in. No step in sight. Was she to climb on the wheel? She raised her brows and lifted a shoulder. Perhaps the axle?

She glanced at Tommy, whose freckles suddenly stood out on reddened cheeks.

"Oh, sorry, ma'am." He wound the reins around

the wooden brake handle then jumped down. He dashed to her side and placed his foot up on the axle. "Just step here and put your other foot right on the floor there, by the seat, and in you go."

Emily studied him from the corner of her eyes, then gauged the distance from the ground to where his foot rested. Hmm. She wasn't sure her skirt would allow that kind of step, not unless she hiked the hem above her knees. She bit back a smile. Now that would make a fine entrance to her new home.

Well. She wouldn't know until she tried. She thrust her reticule at Tommy and carefully lifted her foot. Sure enough, the hem started to slide up. White petticoat ruffles peeped out. How did the women of Wylder mount these blasted wagons?

She extended her leg farther until her ankle showed. She lowered her foot.

"Looks like that pretty outfit you're wearing wasn't made for Western riding."

"Oh!" She started at the soft, raspy voice. The man in the red shirt stood at her side, leading his horse. He swung the saddle down and dropped the reins to the ground. The horse stood in place.

"This will be faster."

Before she could utter a sound, he'd grasped her around her waist and swung her up onto the seat.

Never, ever, had a strange man put a hand on her body unless to dance. For an instant, Emily sat speechless. Breathless. Warmth stung her cheeks. The pressure of his fingers tingled through layers of cloth.

Should she thank him for his help, or scold him for his scandalous action?

Tommy had no doubts. He scurried back to his

place on the seat. "Thanks for your help, mister," he said. "That solved the problem right quick."

Emily couldn't force her eyes from the stranger's gaze. Compelling, questioning.

He touched the brim of his hat and gave a short nod. "Ma'am. You're welcome."

His right eyelid dipped and he walked away, taking her breath and a good part of her sanity with him. She couldn't make out what had just happened. Except the rascal had winked, cool as you please. Should she be insulted? Angry? Embarrassed? Oh! She'd neglected to thank him. Now she *was* embarrassed.

David had a lot to explain. *And I have a lot to learn*. Much more than she'd imagined.

Tommy unwrapped the reins, unlocked the brake, and the horse clopped forward.

"Where to, ma'am?"

She straightened her back, firmed her shoulders, and waved her hand in front of her nose to dispel engine fumes. "The newspaper office, please."

The reins jerked, and the horse stopped. The youth's face beamed red again.

"That wouldn't be such a good idea, ma'am."

Chapter 3

Morgan's fingers tingled from handling the lady. Funny how, through the layers of cloth and corset and petticoats and all the other fripperies proper ladies wore, her warmth had burned his hands. And he'd swear a faint, sweet fragrance wafted around her. Like flowers. He was a fool. She'd obviously been riding the train for days. The fragrance was more likely train smoke.

Still, he'd been tempted to brush his nose against her neck, pull her against him instead of lift her away. Inhale her sweetness and forget all else.

His body hardened. He hadn't come across a lady like her in a long time. Something about her intrigued him. Her blushes, her guarded glances, her breathless words. Yet she possessed a calm confidence. All that combined to tickle his fancy.

It's all in your mind, Morgan my boy. Trouble was he had a vivid imagination. And it usually got him in trouble.

Not this time.

He tried to recall his agreeable bedmate of last night—Connie, Cora, something with a C. He ought to be satisfied for a while after her performance. A cattle drive didn't offer much chance to meet females, unless it passed close enough to a town for the men to get a night off. Didn't happen often. He'd grown used to long periods without a woman. Might not like it, but a man could tolerate anything for a while if he saw an end coming.

Last night, he'd made up for a damn long stretch of patience.

Lord knew he'd seen the misery a female could put a man through. He'd lost a couple of friends that way. One to the bottle and the other to a damned mean streak that left him lying in the dust of a Texas street.

That's why Morgan never bothered with females like the lady in blue. They lived in a different world from his, and the two never intersected. Ladies like her meant marriage, permanence. Two things Morgan had spent the last dozen years avoiding.

Except— His horse tossed its head, reminding him to pay attention. He tightened his hands around the reins. "Easy, Brag."

He led the bay to the hitching rail in front of Wylder's depot, then tossed the saddle across the blanket covering the animal's back. With an easy efficiency learned from his father lifetimes ago, he tightened straps and gave the warm, glowing hide a pat.

A sudden motion at the edge of his vision made him tense. Just the buckboard with the pretty lady in blue making a quick stop. The boy driving said something to her, a look of dismay on his face.

Not my problem. Morgan loosened his muscles and made ready to meet his new employer. Another fellow passenger from this morning, but not as pleasant as the lady. The man didn't need to be. He just needed to provide a place to sleep and the wage he'd promised. If the job lasted too long, Morgan would winter in Wylder, then head out as soon as the passes cleared next spring.

He strode into the depot. Stopping at the clerk's window, he asked, "Mr. Foster?"

"Next door." The clerk nodded toward an open door along the back wall. "Name? I'll tell him you're here."

"Don't bother. He's expecting me." Morgan moved quietly to the opening. A few paces across the packed earth sat another, bigger building. "Rail Offices" was painted in black on a sign swinging above a door.

Hearing nothing from the other side, he tried the latch. He found Foster gazing out the window toward the buckboard, now bouncing along the rutted path to the street.

He waited.

****

Eli Foster had hurried into his office and laid his briefcase on the desk that took up a good third of the tiny room. In two strides he was at the window. Outside, the lady from the train sat beside the boy from the livery stable. What was his name—Tommy, that was it. Seemed like they were disagreeing about something. She didn't look angry, just insistent. Tommy looked miserable.

He leaned closer. *Damned dirty glass*. He took a handkerchief from his pocket and rubbed grime from the window. His lip curled at the black smudges on the white square. Hadn't anybody bothered to clean in here the entire time he was gone? Lazy bastards.

Visibility improved, he lowered his head for a better view. She was a looker. Soft chestnut curls, snapping hazel eyes. That blue outfit she wore, with the white ruffles round the throat and at the wrists—he'd seen get-ups just like that in Washington D.C. And that hat, with the bows and ribbons. Nothing to match it in Wylder. No female here could afford it. He'd had occasion to buy a lady's hat when he was in New York. The thing had cost more than a good bull calf.

She was a *lady*, all right.

Looked like the argument was settled, because Tommy lifted the reins, and the horse clopped ahead. *Who the hell is she, and why is she way out here?*

"Jed." His shout was pitched loud enough to carry over to the depot, beyond the closed door. Except when he turned, he saw it wasn't closed. And a cowboy stood in front of the desk. Tall, wearing a gun. The man in the red shirt from the train. *Damn, how did he sneak in?*

The station clerk poked his head around the corner of the doorframe. "Yes, sir?"

Eli's attention snapped back. "Send a message to the livery. Tell Tommy I want to see him."

The clerk disappeared, and Eli sauntered to his chair, gaze moving over the waiting stranger. "Morgan Dodd?"

"That's right."

Eli nodded. "You made good time. Close the door and sit."

While Dodd shut the door and pulled up one of the two wooden chairs, Eli evaluated the cowboy's movements. Easy, economical, quiet. And he never once showed Eli his back.

Cautious. He liked cautious.

He didn't like smart. Smart meant thinking, and thinking meant trouble. The last man he'd hired had thought too much for his own good. *Devil take Bobby.* Eli wouldn't make that mistake again.

Dodd sat still as he waited, contained. Yet energy pulsed through the air. Eli studied him. The silence stretched, broken now and then by a muffled sound from outside. The cowboy's face remained blank, but Eli had a distinct feeling the man found the staredown amusing. It lay in the glint of his eyes.

Finally, Eli tipped his head. "I've heard good things about you. That land, ah…misunderstanding… down in Texas."

Dodd raised his eyebrows. "Which one?"

Eli chuckled and shifted in his chair. Why in hell couldn't the man show some emotion, so Eli could tell what he was thinking? Such a trait was handy in a shootist, though. "Around the Staked Plains?"

"It got worked out."

"Last job?"

"Scouting and some hunting for the Ranley drive. Made Cheyenne day before yesterday."

"I wasn't expecting you until next week, but it's good you're early," Eli said. "Couldn't have worked out better."

He scribbled a note and held it out. "Give this to Ray Horton. He's my foreman. Take the road west of town about thirty minutes, you'll come to the ranch. The Bar F."

Dodd rose and pocketed the folded paper. "Orders?"

"Something's come up I want you to handle soon as possible. Need to find a former ranch hand who's been stealing from me and others around here. I fired him, of course, but that just set him off more. He's gonna kill somebody if he's not stopped.

"I'll be out to talk to the men later in the week. I'll

have details for you then. Meanwhile, take your lead from Ray."

When Dodd didn't move, Eli stood. "Well?"

"I usually get half the pay up front, the second half when the job's done."

He narrowed his eyes. Half payment, like hell. Who did this drifter think he was? "I don't work that way."

Dodd sat. "Then neither do I."

Eli clenched his teeth and looked down at the damned cowboy. He'd leaned back and propped an ankle on the opposite knee. Eli might have the position of authority standing over the fellow, still a streak of uncertainty twitched up his spine. The feeling angered him.

He ought to dismiss the nervy bastard right now. But the cool disinterest of the other man got to him, and he recalled why he'd hired Morgan Dodd in the first place. The man had made a name for himself. He got the job done with a minimum of trouble, meaning the minimum of deaths. And that meant a minimum of questions from whatever law happened to circulate in the area. A handy talent. God knew Eli didn't need questions. Finally, he said, "A quarter in advance."

Dodd's foot thudded on the plank floor, and he unfolded up. "A third, in cash."

The easy movements, the blank face, the soft voice...Eli shrugged. "A third, then. But you damn well better be worth the trouble."

He stepped to the safe in one corner. Blocking the controls with his body—he intended to remain the only one who knew the combination—he dialed the numbers. The door swung ajar, and he opened a box on the top shelf to count out the cash. He turned and held out a stack of bills. "Three hundred. Now get out before I change my mind."

Dodd took the bills and nodded. "I'll be waiting."

Eli closed the safe, then strolled to the window to contemplate his latest hire. Outside, the gunman gathered the reins of a handsome bay gelding waiting patiently at the hitching post. An effortless swing had the man in the saddle. He reined the horse around into a walk toward the center of town.

Had hiring him been a mistake? More gun muscle might not be needed, now that Eli's most vocal threat, the newspaper editor, had been removed. And it looked like Bobby had left off interfering in his plans, but the traitor needed to be got rid of.

Oh, well. Eli would keep Dodd on until after the election. Then he'd see.

At the desk, he opened the briefcase he'd brought from his trip East and slid out a sheaf of papers. He'd worked through them all, and still the boy from the livery hadn't appeared. He shoved back his chair, his temper as sharp as the crimp between his shoulders. Damn insolent kid—probably wasting time around the horses instead of answering Eli's summons.

Before he could bellow for the ticket clerk again, a pounding sounded at the door.

"Come in," he shouted.

Tommy popped in, cap clutched in hand. "You wanted to see me, sir?"

"I did. You must have come by way of Cheyenne."

The youth cringed at Eli's irascible tone, and Eli sucked in a breath. Nothing to be gained by railing against Tommy.

"Sorry for taking so long, sir. The lady had some chores for me afore I come back."

"I see." Eli forced a benign smile and assumed a jolly if strained tone. "Understandable, young man. Sit down. I see you have a new job, driving the livery stable's buckboard. Well done. Any problems so far?"

Tommy's eyes widened "No, sir." He fidgeted in his chair, as if expecting a further scold.

"I was on the train today, along with a stranger, a lady. She was your passenger. I didn't catch her name when we were introduced. Did she find her relatives at home?"

"Oh, sir. She's Miss Martin, the newspaper editor's sister. Don't know what she's gonna do now."

Chapter 4

"Oh, dear heaven," Emily whispered.

She fought to suck in a breath. Her lungs refused to cooperate.

There must be some mistake.

She stood in the center of the one large room comprising the newspaper office. And turned in a circle. Again.

The office of *The Wylder Sun* lay in chaos.

Only the swish of skirts and the slide of shoes interrupted the silence.

At last her throat opened, and she gasped.

"David can't be gone."

"Sorry, ma'am. It's the God's truth," The boy— Tommy—assured her. "A good two weeks now it's been."

A corner of her mind still hoped it might all be a joke. Her brother loved to tease.

But no. He'd never allow this disaster.

"Are you all right, Miss Martin? Ma'am?" Tommy stood just inside the open door. When she didn't answer, he took a few steps forward. "Want to go to Mr. Martin's house now? Not much to be done here."

"Tell me again what happened," she said, voice choked. "And when."

The boy rubbed the back of his neck. "Two Fridays past, it was. Right after the weekly paper got printed.

Mr. Martin come to the livery stable, saddled his horse, and rode out. Couldn't see which way he went once he got to Wylder Street."

"And you didn't see him come back?"

"Nobody seen him since. Charlie said when he come in the next Monday morning, he found the place like this."

Charlie was the typesetter, Emily recalled from David's letters.

"Where does Charlie live?"

"He lives over to Culpepper's Boarding House, but he's not been around since then either. He might of gone to Cheyenne. His brother works at a newspaper there."

Emily continued to survey the scene around her. Bright light through the front window fell in wavy streaks across the littered floor. The large desk was upended, three chairs overturned and a fourth nothing but kindling, papers scattered everywhere, books dumped in front of shelves along one wall. She righted a chair and sank onto it.

This all must have happened after David left. But why would he disappear without word? His last letter said he was on to an important story.

"Perhaps he decided to follow up on a lead," she murmured.

"Ma'am?"

But if he planned to leave, he would have telegraphed her, told her to postpone her visit. His last letter contained only the vague reference to that mysterious investigation and descriptions of his small house. *Looking forward to your arrival, sister*, he'd ended.

She sucked in yet another deep breath then pressed her hand against her chest. Heartbeat calming. Good. Now she had to think.

The printing press!

She shot up and picked a path through the debris.

At the back of the room, typeset boxes had been upended, with upper case and lower case letters twined across the floor. Something heavy—a mallet perhaps?—had been taken to the plates, bending even those pieces of heavy metal.

As for the press—she couldn't tell if it was terminally damaged or simply dismantled. Her brother liked the ancient Stanhope, the flat-bed printing easier for a pair of men to handle than newer models.

Oh, David. She surreptitiously dashed away tears then turned.

The boy shifted from foot to foot. "Ready to go?" His nervous voice urged her to hurry.

"Very well. Take me to Mr. Martin's house, and we'll unload my baggage. Then I would like you to bring me back here."

His mouth, twisted uncertainly to the side, showed just what he thought of that idea. But apparently he'd been raised right and simply nodded. "Yes, ma'am. If'n that's what you'd like."

Fortunately, David's house sat on the first street behind the main town, a short distance from the *Sun*. She could walk back and forth to the office. No need to worry about transportation. *Good.*

While Tommy brought her luggage inside, Emily did a quick walk-through of the rooms. Perhaps David had left some message. She found nothing. Tonight she'd search the place thoroughly.

Some twenty minutes later, she again stood in the middle of the newspaper office after bidding goodbye to Tommy. The office was a single large room, divided in half on one side by tall, wide, wooden bookshelves. Judging from the debris surrounding them, they were used for storage. She roamed the space, checking shelves, nudging bundles of paper with her toe. In the back corner opposite the press, a partition rose mid-way to the ceiling. What looked like a sheet served as a door.

Hesitantly, she drew back the fabric. Tucked inside—a cot, a stand with an empty pitcher and bowl, and peeping from under the cot, a chamber pot. Her brother's quarters on nights he didn't make it home from the paper.

What should she do? Question the authorities, certainly. Oh, and check at the bank, to see if he'd made a withdrawal before he left. She must leave her name at the post office. Her mother undoubtedly planned to write immediately.

Feeling nominally better now she had at least three objectives, she started for the door.

"First, the bank." The soft sound of her whisper filled the silence, somehow reassuring. She paused. Best to ask questions while conducting business. She meant to open an account, anyway. Her oversized reticule bag held a letter of credit from her family's bank in Kansas City. Her father would ship her funds with Wells Fargo once the account was opened.

Reluctant to depend on credit or on David's generosity for her pin money until that time, however, she'd come prepared. She slipped behind the curtain then unbuttoned her long, fitted bodice. Thread at the top of her corset lining had been removed, and inside the resulting pockets between stays lay six flattened fifty dollar greenbacks.

Her father would never have allowed her to travel alone had he known she'd brought along cash in this way. But what did it matter? No one could tell.

After the front-lacing corset was retied and her bodice in place, Emily slipped the bills inside her reticule and set out.

To the right of the *Sun* building sat the sheriff's office. Why hadn't she noticed it earlier? The location certainly hadn't discouraged the vandals who destroyed the newspaper.

She swerved onto the wooden walk and opened the door. Inside at a desk sat a young man, too young for the badge pinned to his shirt. "Sheriff?"

He looked up. "Not here, ma'am. Can I help you?"

Emily considered the question, then smiled. "No thank you. I'll come back."

She wanted to face the sheriff when she asked what had been done to investigate her brother's disappearance. And why the devil someone hadn't heard the *Sun* being wrecked and stopped it.

Outside she paused to look around. On a building across the street, huge letters painted across the front identified Goldmount Bank.

Thank goodness. She glanced to the left for oncoming horses or carriages, then smiled as she realized what she'd done. Not likely a freight wagon would lumber around a corner and threaten to run everyone down. Across the street, a handful of horses stood outside the bank, a group of men clustered on the wooden walk in front of them. A horse and buggy had been tied to a hitching post just down from the sheriff's office. A woman with a young girl at her side turned into a doorway, but Emily couldn't make out the name of the store.

After the bank, she'd take a walk around town to familiarize herself. Perhaps find a café.

A few long, curious looks followed her across the street. She had just gained the plank walk when a passing cowboy stopped, backtracked a few steps, and opened the bank's door for her. He touched the wide brim of his hat and nodded as she murmured, "Thank you."

Inside, a long counter with a lone customer window fronted a space containing three desks. In a back corner loomed a huge iron safe. A man with a rifle across his knees sat near it, a large tin coffee cup on a table at his elbow.

In front of her at the customer window stood a man in a red calico shirt. The shirt alone would have been a giveaway, but the straight broad shoulders and the slight tilt of his head confirmed the identity of the man wearing it. Her throat tightened, and her stomach plunged. The cowboy from the train. She brushed a hand across her waist where the remembered imprint of his fingers took up throbbing.

Head lowered, he slid a folded piece of paper into his shirt pocket as he turned. His gaze collided with hers. A tiny smile lifted one side of his expressive mouth, and he touched his hat brim. "Ma'am."

Emily's lips curved upward in an answering greeting before she realized what she'd done. Flattening her mouth, she nodded. Heat flooded her face.

Good heavens. Blushing because a handsome

stranger spoke to her—what was this, the third time today? She was acting like a ninny, not a woman used to greeting scores of gentlemen at her parents' gatherings. Not someone experienced in debating women's issues at public meetings. And certainly not like an author of a weekly opinion column for the *Kansas City Times*.

Confidence restored, she tilted her chin and stepped forward to the window.

"May I speak with the manager?"

The clerk turned to the man seated at one of the desks behind him. The man nodded without bothering to look up.

The clerk stepped to the side and opened the gate to the back. "This is Mr. Willard."

Smiling her thanks, she approached the desk, and the man rose. Not much taller than she, he had thin blond hair receding in the front, and eyebrows creased in a look of permanent consternation.

"Good morning, Mr. Willard," she said, "I would like to open an account."

"Of course." He gestured to a chair beside the desk. His actions were polite, his expression admiring. "You just sit right here, ma'am. I don't believe I've seen you in town before. Are you visiting?" He looked toward the door. "Will your husband be joining you?"

Resisting the temptation to roll her eyes, she adopted her polite-but-business-y tone. "I am Miss Emily Martin. I have just arrived in town, and I wish to open an account of my own."

She placed her bag on the corner of the desk and opened the drawstring. "My brother is David Martin. I believe he also banks here."

The admiration slid into surprise then pity. "Has no one told you, Miss Martin? Your brother has...that is, he's..."

"Not in town at the moment?" She completed the sentence he'd left dangling. "So I've learned. Now, about my account. Here is a letter of credit from my home bank. Will you be prepared to receive additional funds on my behalf?"

She met Mr. Willard's surprised stare. "You do accept shipments from Wells Fargo, do you not?"

"Certainly." He glanced at the letter she handed him, then fumbled with some papers in a drawer, sliding a sheet to the surface.

The poor man. She supposed she should have approached him differently, but it was too late now. Surely other women maintained personal accounts. David had assured her that the people of Wylder were open minded and that several females operated their own businesses.

She withdrew the fifty-dollar bills from her bag and handed them over. Then retrieved one. "I'll need to purchase supplies for the house."

As the manager filled out the account records, she leaned forward slightly to follow his progress on the page. "I'll be living with my brother while I visit, of course, so please use his address."

His hand hovered above the sheet, and he frowned.

"He will be back very soon." She only wished she felt as confident as she sounded. Her entire insides quivered with nerves. Blast it. Somewhere between stepping through the bank doors and sitting in this chair, events of the day had begun to sink in.

Finally, the manger laid aside his pen. "Miss

Martin—"

"Sir," she interrupted, launching an offensive. "I've been told my brother rode out of town one Friday afternoon and never returned. I would like to know if he withdrew an amount from his account before he left."

The manager's face flushed as deep pink as her mother's favorite cabbage roses. "I can't discuss details of customer accounts," he said. She stood, and he followed suit. "That is private."

"Please understand," Emily softened her tone. "I'm not asking the amount, just whether he made a withdrawal." His mouth puckered. Oh, dear, she should have behaved with a bit less independence. Eyes lowered, she considered a moment. She hated like the devil to do this, but she feared she'd be here all afternoon trying to reason with the man otherwise. So she allowed tears to fill her eyes and her mouth to tremble.

"That way," she murmured, "perhaps I'll know if he forgot I was to visit. If he planned to be gone for days, then perhaps I should just go home."

"Now, Miss Martin, ma'am, don't cry." He hurried around to her side. "I'm sure he couldn't forget you were coming. Don't you listen to what some people say. He's bound to be back before long."

He gestured to the clerk. "Joe, did the newspaper editor take out any money before he left?"

The clerk pulled out a ledger and flipped through a few pages, then shook his head. "Nope. No record of it."

"There, you see? He must not plan to be away long at all. Don't you worry. He'll turn up soon."

"Thank you, sir," Emily said. She sniffed, then

gave him a wavery smile. "If I could have my deposit record, I'll leave now. Oh, and may I have some smaller bills?" She handed him the fifty-dollar bill she'd retained. "There's a café in town, isn't there?"

"The ladies like the Wylder Side Bakery, right across the street," he said, handing the money to the clerk. "Joe here will get you fixed up and point you in the right direction."

After another thank you to both the manager and Joe, who handed over her change, Emily left the bank. Just across the street she spied the bakery. Thank goodness.

Chapter 5

Morgan set his cup of coffee and plate of cherry pie on the lone table in the bakery shop and dropped onto a chair. Been a long time since he'd seen home cooking like the pie sitting in front of him.

He tried a bite. His eyes drifted closed as he savored the tart fruit, the sweet custard, the crisp flaky crust. Damn good. It was his secret, this love of dessert. He didn't often get a chance to indulge it. His mother had made biscuits as light and sweet as cake and her strawberry jam—ambrosia.

His throat tightened. He hadn't thought of his mother's cooking in years. He forced his mind from his childhood to his new job. And new employer. What did the man have planned? Morgan usually knew what was expected of him before he ever signed on, and he never took a job that flat out called for murder. He knew how to use a gun. Didn't mean he was a killer. Most jobs dealt with border disputes or cattle thieving. He didn't hold with attacking homesteaders to drive them out. Brought back too many bad memories.

It was a morning for memories. Maybe that's what had him thinking too much. He ought to just eat his pie and head out to the ranch. Think of the future, not the past.

Trouble was he didn't trust Foster any farther than he could toss Brag. The man was too changeable.

Affable one minute, like his conversation with the lady on the train, then sharp and manipulative, like when he'd greeted Morgan in his office.

Sure, men treated ladies and men, especially employees, different. But Foster's behavior toward the lady this morning went beyond affable. It was...his mother used to have a word for that. Oh, yes. Unctuous.

The image of the lady in blue lingered in his mind. She was the prettiest thing he'd seen in years. But she wasn't just pretty, she had a way about her. He liked the confidence of her walk, the straight set of her shoulders, and the slight tilt of her head, as if she puzzled out every new thing she saw.

Most of all, she possessed an air of eagerness, of anticipation. As if she intended to meet the world head on.

Had he ever been young enough, innocent enough, to welcome a new day? A picture of the farm flickered into his mind. Sunday mornings, Mother and Dad waiting for him at the buggy.

He shoved the image back to the dark confines of memory. What the hell had come over him today? He didn't have time for sentiment. Sentimental fools died early.

Still, thoughts of the lady refused to go away. Shame he didn't know her name. Not that it would do a damn bit of good. The gulf between them was as big as the Rio Grande. And what the hell was he doing, mooning over a woman right now? He had a job to do, money to earn, a new start to look forward to. Maybe in California he'd be able to settle down.

The woman who'd served him came around the counter, holding the tall tin coffee pot. "Warm up?

How's the pie?"

"Best thing I've tasted in I don't know when." He held up the cup. "Wish I could take a whole one with me, but I doubt it would make the trip."

"New to town, are you? Where you headed?"

"I'm working for Eli Foster, out at his ranch."

The stream of coffee missed the cup and splattered the table. The woman stepped back. "Goodness me, I'm sorry. Here, let me get something to clean that up." She disappeared into the back of the shop, but her voice carried out. "So you're the new hand at the Bar F. Heard he was hiring."

She reappeared with a square of toweling and mopped the tabletop. "There we are. Sorry again. I didn't catch your name."

Before he could speak, the door opened, and the lady from the train stepped in. *What the hell?* This was what, the third time he'd run into her since they arrived in Wylder this morning? Not that he minded.

She didn't glance around but went straight to the front. The woman from the counter rushed up, a friendly smile. The two exchanged words. Morgan couldn't hear their low tones, not that he was listening. They laughed, then the lady turned, holding a plate with cherry pie in one hand and a cup in the other.

"We have just the one table," the other woman said. "You can share with this gentleman, can't you? He's new to town too."

The lady in blue's gaze met his and she raised her brows. Looked like she recognized him.

A moment of silence stretched awkwardly. Finally, he smiled. "That pie you're holding is mighty good. If you don't mind joining me...I'll be leaving soon."

"Thank you." He could swear a look of uncertainty crossed her face, then she glanced at his plate. In a bright but controlled tone, she said, "The pie does look delicious."

She set her dishes on the table and lowered to the only other chair. Well, damn. He should have risen and pulled it out for her. Just showed how long he'd been outside civilization. His soft, disgusted, "Hunh," nearly blotted out her long sigh.

He cut her a quick glance. "Pardon me, ma'am. Are you all right? I couldn't help notice you might be having problems earlier."

A startled expression widened her eyes, and her teeth found the edge of her lower lip. The expression was replaced by an uncertain frown. After a moment, she said, "Just getting settled in. Thank you."

Her attention returned to her food, and she seemed to draw into herself. Obviously she wasn't interested in talking. He finished his coffee and stood. The counter lady came to pick up his dishes. She carried a cloth-wrapped object.

"Mighty good, ma'am. Thanks." He started for the door.

"Just a minute." She held out the package. "Here's a slice of that pie to take along. Bring back my pie tin next time you're in town. Good luck to you."

Morgan found himself at the hitching post before the surprise faded. Damn fine woman, that cook. He slid the pie into the top of his pack and mounted Brag. Time to get to work.

****

Through the bakery window, Emily watched the cowboy ride away. Something about him still robbed her of breath—and rational thought. Him with his wrinkled shirt and forward manner. She wasn't used to men having such an effect on her. Even Randolph hadn't made her stomach lurch like this, and all her friends at home considered him a handsome man. Randolph. Hah. Handsome is as handsome does. And it did pretty poorly by him.

The chair opposite her scraped the floor, and the counter lady sat down. "Mind if I join you for a sip of coffee?" She put her cup on the table.

Emily sat back in her chair, surprised at the woman's action.

The attractive woman smiled. She was young, Emily realized. About her own age. "I'm Cissy Standish. This is my place. Just arrived in town, have you?"

The West is friendlier. Emily remembered that from David's words. She'd best get used to it. She nodded. "I'm Emily Martin and yes, I came in on the morning train."

"Martin? David's sister? He's told me a lot about you. Last time he was in, he said you might be visiting. I'm glad to meet...." The sentence trailed off, and Cissy's eyes lost their merry glint. She reached over to grasp Emily's hand resting on the table. "You've heard, haven't you? Mrs. Dikes was in a short while ago with her daughter, and she said a livery buckboard was parked outside the *Sun*."

The lively chatter, the immediate acceptance, the fact David had spoken of her to this friendly woman *the last time he was in* suddenly overwhelmed Emily. The brittle shield she'd erected around herself in the last hours cracked. Everything around her became wavy—

Cissy, the food on the table, the counter. She blinked rapidly and forced a tingling lump down her throat. *I will not cry.* She clenched her teeth and gave a sharp, jerky nod.

Cissy squeezed Emily's hand and threw her a challenging look. "You plan to stay, don't you?"

What could she say? "I don't know," she admitted, her voice low. "I haven't had a great deal of time to think things through."

Cissy nodded. "Feeling numb, I bet. And stranded. I know the feeling well. When I came to Wylder, things were hard for me too."

This happy, confident woman once faced difficulties here? Impossible to believe.

"Then I met my husband, Buck, and after we married, he helped me start the bakery. So don't give up."

In spite of the uncertain situation, she had to smile. It wavered. "I don't intend to meet a man, wonderful or otherwise."

"Aha!" Cissy finished off her coffee. "I hear a story there. Next time you drop by, maybe you'd like to tell me about it?"

Emily picked up her fork and met the other woman's friendly gaze. "Perhaps."

Cissy rose. "That's the spirit. I have to clean up the stove and oven in the back. If you need anything, give a holler."

The pie melted on her tongue and for a moment, she simply enjoyed the food and the coffee. Strong, hot. Just as she liked it. She heard the creak and squeal of a heavy wagon on the street, the muffled thud of horses' hooves. It sounded strangely isolated, and for a moment, Emily felt suspended in a vacuum. Alone.

She shivered, and a streak of fear burned through her.

No. No fear. She was on her own, just as she'd wanted. She could do this.

The watch pinned to the left side of her bodice showed nearly one p.m. With a slow deep breath, she considered what to do next. Visit the post office, then back to David's house, check supplies.

Seven days before the next train to Cheyenne. Seven days to decide her future. Return to her parents' house or remain in Wylder to wait for David? Her mind veered away from the choice, and she rose. "Mrs. Standish, I'm leaving now. The pie was absolutely delicious. Thank you."

"Call me Cissy, Emily." Cissy stuck her head around the corner of the door, a dishtowel in her hand. "If you need anything, let me know. I'll help in any way I can."

The kind offer caused Emily's throat to tighten and tingle again. No matter what happened after today, she felt as if she'd found a friend.

Chapter 6

Outside the bakery, Emily stood for a moment to get her bearings. She recalled seeing the post office sign this morning, on the other side of the depot. Not all that far to walk. Directly across the street lay what looked like a sizeable lane between buildings. It should take her in the right direction. Slipping the loop of her reticule over her left arm, she set out.

An outdoor theatre anchored the corner to her left and on her right, Lowery Dress Shop. Midway, Jake's Place sat to her left. A restaurant. Thank heavens.

She reached the end of the lane to find two saloons flanked her. She'd never before ventured past saloons. No one lingered outside either building, so she had no reason for nerves to start up. A team of mules pulling a large empty wagon was the only traffic on the wider street she faced.

The depot sat directly in front of her, and there was the post office, two doors down. Once the wagon passed, she crossed.

A postal clerk looked up when she entered. "Afternoon," he said.

"Good afternoon. I'm Emily Martin. I'll be visiting in town for a few weeks. I wanted to introduce myself so when my mail arrives, you'll know who to save it for."

"Well, now, that's a right good idea," the clerk

said. "Martin…Martin. Relation to David Martin, the newspaper fella?

"He's my brother."

"Uh, huh." The man squinted at her, his tone a suspicious neutral. "Plan to stay awhile, do you?"

"A few weeks, until my brother gets back. He's on a short trip."

"Uh, huh." The clerk squatted behind the counter, leaving Emily a view of brown hair thinning around a bald spot. He stood and held out an envelope between his forefinger and thumb. "Thought I had something here. Somebody's expecting you."

Unexpected familiarity gave her a warm wash of relief. Mother must have sent a welcome note before Emily left Kansas City.

"Thank you." She smiled and took the mail from his hand—nails clean, she noted, although his skin was cracked and stained brown. "My mother. A welcome to the new home. She did the same…" Emily almost said, "When I moved to school," but stopped. That would sound pretentious. Not a good way for folks here to think of her.

"She did the same the last time I was away from home." She shook her head. "Mothers. They never stop treating us as children."

"Wouldn't know. My ma died when I was two."

Oh, dear. Heat burned Emily's cheeks. She'd meant the remark to be friendly, not hurtful. "I'm so sorry," she murmured.

He gave a jerk of his head. "Ain't nothing."

"Thank you for keeping this for me, Mr…"

"Jasper." He scratched his cheek with his forefinger, nail rasping against beard stubble.

"Thank you, Mr. Jasper."

"No Mister, just Jasper." He leaned forward, forearms on the counter. "What's gonna happen with the paper while your brother's away? Gonna have somebody clean up that office and put out the news?"

She paused, hand suspended in mid-air. Publish the paper herself? Panic had her heart pounding. She'd promised David to help with the writing. He was the expert on the technical side of newspapering.

"I don't know, Mr., that is, Jasper. I arrived this morning. I haven't had a chance to decide."

"Uh, huh. Well, if'n you do, just remember to get any papers to mail here afore three on Fridays, so's I'll have time to get 'em ready for Saturday."

Emily slipped the envelope into her reticule and stepped outside. Into a different world. In the few minutes she'd been in the post office, the streets had filled. Three horses stood at a hitching rail in front of the saloon on one corner across from her. A group of laughing, cursing men shouldered through the swinging doors of the saloon on the other corner. Riders threaded into the lane she'd traveled, toward Jake's probably, and a dust cloud settled as a buggy pulled in next door. A woman approached the post office carrying a package. Emily stepped aside and returned the woman's friendly smile.

Rounding the corner onto a street at her right was a buckboard. From this distance the driver looked like the youth who had helped her earlier. Livery stable must be that way. Maybe the owner would have a horse and buggy to rent if she needed them. She'd follow Tommy.

Emily sucked in a deep breath and coughed. Waving dust away from her face, she blanked her mind to the problems awaiting and headed after the buckboard. Thank goodness the distance wasn't far.

Yes, she learned, the livery did have rigs and horses for rent. Relieved she'd have transportation if needed, Emily finally made it back home. The quiet of David's house teased her tired ears when she stepped through the front door. Peace. She set her reticule down and sank into a chair. Elbows on the table, she rested her head in her hands. And the events of the last hours crashed around her ears.

What on earth was going on? David was gone— where? The newspaper was wrecked—why? She sat alone in a Western town—the distant sound of two quick gunshots made her jump and jerk up her head.

"What—?" Heart pounding, she leapt to her feet and raced to the window in the front room.

No one outside. The shots must have come from town, which really was only a street away. Had anyone been hurt? Good heavens. This all felt as if she were trapped in a dime novel.

What was she doing here? Emily began to laugh, the sound loud and harsh in the otherwise empty room. As the laughter changed, she covered her face with her hands. Tears seeped between her fingers. She stumbled back to the table and sat, buried her head in her folded arms, and allowed herself a good cry.

After a few minutes, she fumbled a handkerchief from her reticule, mopped her eyes, and wiped her nose. *Enough of this*. She sat straight and hitched a breath. *Consider the options.*

She could always go home.

Run home.

She didn't like the sound of that. Still, a possibility.

Through the quiet, a sound niggled her ears. Scratching? Not mice! Oh, no! She shot to her feet and dashed into the kitchen. As she neared the back door, the sound grew louder. She paused with a hand on the latch. A tiny, high cry reached her. Cautiously, she opened the door. There on the threshold, big eyes fixed hopefully on Emily, sat a bundle of gray fur.

A tiny kitten. Emily knelt and took it into her hands. The fur masked a thin, hungry body.

"Oh, you poor thing," she murmured. "Are you supposed to be here? David never said a word about a pet."

And he wouldn't leave a kitten to fend for itself if he'd decided to travel. Therefore, it must belong to someone else.

"Where do you live?" The kitten lifted its head with what Emily marked as a hopeful expression.

"Wherever that is, they're not caring for you." Emily cuddled the small animal close and ran her forefinger down the back of its head. A feeling of protectiveness suddenly made her feel more confident. This adorable kitty needed food and some care.

"Would you like to stay with me for a while?" She carried the little mite to the table and sat, placing it before her. It stretched, shook itself, and immediately headed for the pull cords on Emily's reticule.

"No, no. That's not to play with." Laughing, she swooped up the fur ball. "You need food. Let's see what's here." She held it carefully while she rummaged through the pie safe. On a lower shelf she found several cans of condensed milk.

"Ah, ha. Here's your supper." She dug through another cabinet and found a box of kitchen utensils, including a can opener. Before long, she set a bowl of milk on the floor by the back door. "Here you are, kitty."

As the kitten lapped the milk, Emily found a stack of *Suns* on a parlor table. She unfolded a few on the floor beside the milk bowl. Then sighed. "I don't suppose you know what this is for."

She'd have to put kitty outside later.

Emily's stomach rumbled, and she chuckled. "Wonder what else David has to eat. What I'd really like is a cup of tea." Did he possibly have…? She checked the small cabinet next to the safe. Thank goodness, a tin with a few tea leaves. She held to her nose for a sniff. "Old," she declared. "Well, better than nothing, right, kitty?"

Now for hot water. A potbellied stove sat in the kitchen. For warmth, no doubt, although a tea kettle would fit nicely on the round, flat top.

No kettle. A long-handled pan would do. She grabbed one from the pie safe and set it on the table. Next, the fire. In July. Oh, well. Needs must. Outside the back door a wooden box held a stack of splintered wood. With wadded paper, she could start a fire.

Bless David for the metal box of matches she found. While the fire established itself with strips of kindling, she grabbed a bucket from beside the dry sink and headed out the back door to the well. *Please, please don't need priming.* She hooked the bucket over the pump spout and grasped the handle. It resisted briefly, and she sighed with relief. Another two pumps and water poured forth. Once the bucket was full, she returned to the kitchen, filled the pan, and set it on the stove top.

A smile crept out, a little at a time. She'd done it. Thank heavens for vacations at the farm with her grandparents. She could manage these small tasks.

Half an hour later, kitty curled on her lap, she sipped her terrible tea. While it had brewed, she'd prepared a list of supplies. Coffee, sugar, a strainer. Food? Her stomach sank. What had she been thinking?

"Oh, kitty. I can't cook." Why had that detail never occurred to her? She knew how to manage a kitchen, and she did know basics. She'd tried her hand at a few meals, but she could never get the stove damper settings just right, and the fire never seemed to burn evenly. She could make soup, boil vegetables, fry eggs. Those items didn't require a constant temperature. Bitty, their family cook, had once said Emily should marry a man with a comfortable job, for she'd surely need help with the meals.

Mother, Dad, and David had laughed at the joke. Emily knew it wasn't a joke.

Thank heaven for restaurants. She'd seen Jake's Place this afternoon, and the hotel had a dining room. She'd be fine. The Mercantile would have most of the other supplies she needed. It wouldn't hurt to ask about staples, though. Where did one find eggs in Wylder? Fresh milk? Bread? Perhaps Cissy sold bread along with her pastries.

She leaned against the back of the chair, and weariness hit her in an angry wave. Perhaps she'd have a lie-down, rest a bit before returning to the office. Her bodice watch showed a little past three. At least two hours until dinner. With kitty on her arm, she headed for the bedroom.

There she found clean bedding in a dresser drawer.

She spread a sheet over the mattress, placed kitty beside the pillow, then collapsed on the bed. And sat straight up.

"Damn." She pulled out two hatpins, removed the jaunty little hat, and tossed in on the floor. Then she went about removing hairpins. In a matter of moments, her hair lay around her shoulders. She sighed and sank down once more.

No matter how tired she felt, sleep wouldn't come. Worries, decisions, events of the day, all marched across her mind like a parade.

Should she clean the *Sun*'s office and try to put out a paper? Should she return home and await word from David? She certainly wouldn't leave until she talked with the sheriff.

Her restlessness prompted kitty to press a tiny cold nose to Emily's cheek.

"Am I keeping you awake too?" she asked as she smoothed fingers down the kitten's back. "I'm just not sure whether I should stay or go. If I do stay, can I make my own way without help?"

She rolled onto her back and stared toward the ceiling. The actions of the day played across the shadowy expanse as if she were watching her own movements from afar. Chills pinched her shoulders again at the devastation of the broken press and littered office, yet she kept returning to the stranger in the red shirt.

He was like no one she'd ever met before, and she couldn't rid him from her mind. Nor could she deny the way her pulse quickened when she saw him, the way her stomach melted at the sound of his voice. Something inside her responded as if she knew him, identified with his easy stride, responded to his wary half-smile.

She turned restlessly and nestled her cheek against kitty's softness. *Good heavens. I stepped from that train into a different world. And I no longer even know myself.*

Kitty crept onto her chest, sinking small, sharp claws into the fabric of Emily's bodice. She plucked the little one into the air. "Why do I keep thinking of that rumpled drifter? Hmm?"

She nestled kitty on the pillow beside her cheek again. "I've met the governor and congressmen, mayors and attorneys—powerful men and many of them quite handsome."

Yet none of those well-dressed, socially adept examples had affected her the way that lone cowboy had. Long dark eyelashes, piercing gray eyes. Chocolate-colored hair curling against his neck. And the way he moved—loose-limbed, easy.

The gun rode his hip as if it had grown there. As much a part of the whole as the slow smile that lifted one side of his mouth—sometimes teasing, sometimes cynical, always as if he mocked himself.

Next to Emily's ear, kitty purred.

"I know." Her hand stroked the ball of fur. "I can't explain it either."

In the distance the sound of laughing, shouting men was punctuated by a couple of gunshots—three. She tensed; had someone been hurt? Then faint, raucous laughter came again, and she let out a breath. Just some fellows sounding off. In broad daylight? Unbelievable.

The reality of living alone wasn't quite what she'd expected. Of course, she'd expected her brother to be present and that details would take care of themselves.

A feeling of homesickness hit, and she suddenly recalled the letter she'd slipped into her reticule at the post office. Perhaps reading that would help settle her.

She retrieved it. Although nothing appeared on the outside except her own printed name along with the town's, the edges were tucked and sealed in a familiar way. But not that of her mother's. Why had she not noticed earlier?

It can't be. Her heart skipped.

After carefully prying open the paper, she removed the single sheet and immediately checked the signature. She gasped.

David.

Emily rose and walked to the parlor window where she had better light.

Em, (Yes, his typical opening)

Sorry to leave so precipitously. I'm on the trail of a story. Not sure where it will take me. The house is yours to use. Take your meals at Jake's Place or the hotel. See Cissy at the bakery for bread.

Sister, I have kept my mission secret from everyone in Wylder. Important that you do the same. Let them believe what they will until my return. Mother and Father know my whereabouts.

Use this time to practice your newspapering. Charlie will take care of the mechanical details. You write to your heart's content.

Affectionately, your brother,

Divvy

Tears welled in Emily's eyes. Divvy was her childhood nickname for him, back when she was too young to pronounce 'David.' Only he would think to sign himself that way.

She read the message again, then folded it slowly, thoughtfully. What story was he investigating? What in this town could be of such importance to send him off so mysteriously? David did have his quirks and special topics he was passionate about. Just as she did. Women's suffrage for one. And that's why she'd looked forward to being in Wyoming, the only territory—or state—that allowed women to vote.

Little more than three months until November. Three months to rally the women of Wylder to use that right. For David had told her he'd never seen a female cast a ballot at any of the elections—local or county— since he'd been here. He'd taken over the *Sun* three years ago, so he hadn't been present for a national election.

But she would be.

Her heart beat faster, and she found herself smiling.

She could do it.

She *would* do it.

Chapter 7

Morgan arrived at the Bar F with no trouble. The foreman, Ray, cast a resentful eye at him, then grunted as he read Foster's note. He nodded toward a long wooden building. "Bunk in there. Chores all done for the day so get some rest. The boss will likely be out tomorrow with a job. Cookie rings the bell for chow."

Sounded fine to Morgan. Inside the empty bunkhouse, he headed to a corner cot that looked vacant and tossed his hat onto the wooden stand beside it. He rubbed his fingers through his hair and stretched out on the mattress. The restlessness he'd had all day still dogged him. It wasn't his reaction to the little lady in blue. Although he had to admit, she occupied his thoughts way too much since he'd seen her on the train. Couldn't quite get a handle on her.

His mind conjured up a picture of her sitting at his table in the bakery. Confident but uncertain at the same time. Shy but with a friendly smile. Shadows under her fine hazel eyes showed exhaustion. He didn't know a damn thing about her, not even her name. What did it matter? He'd likely never see her again. Even if he did, she wasn't the kind of woman he'd take up with.

Or that would take up with him, for that matter. She was bound for a banker's or a rancher's wife with a fancy two story house where she'd give parties for other ladies in town.

But he recalled her smile, tentative, curious, innocent. She was a fine armful. Just right for a man to dream about.

When he wanted reminding of all he'd never have.

The door slammed open against the rough wall, and a cowboy limped in. White showed at the sides of his short dark hair and streaked through the top like a polecat's. Grunting, he wobbled over to a bunk, three up from Morgan's. Back to him, the man stripped off his gun belt and damp shirt then turned to sit. When he saw Morgan, he jerked and reached for the gun he'd just tossed on the bed.

"Friend," Morgan announced and raised a hand.

"Damn near got yourself shot, *friend.* Don't be lurkin' in the corner like that. You the fellow from Texas they been waitin' for?"

Morgan swung his legs over the side of the bed and sat. "I'm up from Texas. Don't know anybody's been waiting for me."

"Mebbe not. Seems like we had plenty of work lately."

Ray stepped into the open doorway. "Back so soon, Willie?"

The other man shook his head. "That damn horse I been riding. Threw a shoe. Second one in a week. Something's wrong with him or else Blackie ain't gettin' 'em on tight. Had to walk him back from the river. The others went on."

"I'll take a look at him." The foreman stepped out, leaving the door open.

Willie flopped back on his mattress. "I tell you, man ain't made to walk that far in boots."

"Can't dispute you there." Morgan returned the old

53

man's grin. "Name's Morgan Dodd. Were you headed out on a job?"

Willie cut him a sharp glance, then pushed up and limped to the boot jack by the door. "Another damn fool homesteader got his cattle run off Wednesday night." He grunted as he pried the boot loose. "Him, his missus, and kids off to a church meetin'. Didn't know the livestock was gone till the next mornin' at chore time."

His boot thunked against the floor. "I allus said religion was dangerous to a man."

The next boot came off easier, and Willie hopped gingerly back to his bunk. "Boss says as how we need to be good neighbors, so he sent out a crew to look for the stock."

Morgan perked up at the mention of stolen cattle. Maybe this was why he'd been hired, sight unseen. "Rustlers a problem around here?"

"Lately. Seems like a lot of the little ranchers're gettin' hit. We been right busy chasin' after other people's livestock."

"Sounds like the boss is a real Good Samaritan, helping out the sheriff like that. Any luck finding them?"

"Found some cattle, but not those as is stealin' 'em. Hell of it is folks are startin' to look to the boss to get 'em back. We got so many of the crew out searchin' some days, ain't nobody left to tend things here."

Why would Foster want to put himself out like that, doing the sheriff's job? From what he'd heard in Cheyenne, Wylder's sheriff could take care of just about anything.

"Getting a name for himself, the boss?" From his

pocket, Morgan pulled out the makings of a smoke and tilted it toward Willie. Willie shook his head, so Morgan concentrated on rolling his own.

A satisfied groan made him look up. Willie had yanked off both socks and was rubbing his toes. The sour odor of unwashed feet confined in sweaty old boots wafted all the way to Morgan's bunk. Willie brushed his hands together and lay back on his bunk. Shrugging his shoulders a few times, he ground his back into the mattress and relaxed with a guttural sigh of satisfaction.

Morgan struck a light to the cigarette and sat on the edge of his cot, forearms resting on knees, letting the silence stretch.

"That's the thing of it," Willie said finally. "Looks like he's tryin' to do just that. Some of us figure he's lookin' to run for office. Maybe county commissioner. Gettin' folks in his debt for a good deed, lendin' a hand when things turn bad for others... All that good will comes in handy at election time." He grunted and plopped his hat across his eyes. "Hell, what do I know. Don't care. Long as he pays my wage, I'm happy to track down whatever he says."

Morgan stubbed out his smoke and waited for Willie to offer more insight. A low snore warned him there'd be no more right now. He rose and edged to the door. Might as well get acquainted with the layout. Then, too, a lot to think about in what he'd just heard.

Small landholders, the target of rustlers; a good neighbor, helping owners find the cattle. But no thieves ever arrested. Convenient. He'd guess a con, but the cattle were always found and returned to the owners. Willie had said "some" though. Which ranchers' animals weren't found? What happened then?

Stealing stock till a homesteader went broke then buying his spread for pennies was a trick Morgan had seen a half dozen times. Big ranchers wanting to get bigger didn't balk at a little rough business to get folks to sell. He'd been roped into a job like that twice when he was younger, and he wanted no part of it now. Running off honest folks trying to make a better life for themselves was the opposite of what Morgan believed in. He hadn't taken another job like that.

But this sounded different. If the cattle were being found and returned to the owners, then nothing appeared underhanded. A man who'd set his whole crew to helping others wasn't likely to be crooked. Trouble was, he'd met Foster, and his opinion of the man didn't mesh with that of a Good Sam. This operation would bear some looking into.

Chapter 8

Emily greeted the sunrise with renewed energy and a long list of projects. First, she'd find out where Charlie had taken a job in Cheyenne, then rent a buggy from the livery stable. Better to speak with him in person rather than to telegraph. She'd certainly need him to set type.

She clenched her eyes shut for a moment at the thought of the wrecked office waiting to be cleaned. But no. Deal with that later. Now, positive steps.

After bathing quickly in cool water poured in a pretty clay pottery basin in the bedroom, she used her toothpowder, donned a simple, tuck-pleated white bodice with close sleeves, then her favorite skirt, dark blue with a modest ruffle that rose to an inverted V in the back. Easy to move in. Thank heavens, bustles were finally out of style.

She twisted her long hair into a knot at her nape and picked up a matching hat. Blue as well, its upturned sides emphasized the downward front curve. With the brim edged in black, it sported a cluster of dark blue ribbon-bows on the left side. She pinned it on. There. Neat, simple but professional.

Breakfast at the hotel, then to work. She poured condensed milk for kitty and set it outside.

"Come now, kitty," she called, closing the back door as kitty shot outside. "Play until I come home."

She sucked in a wavery breath and paused. Lifting her chin, she inhaled deeply once more and set out.

After breakfast, she rented a horse and buggy at the livery and learned at which Cheyenne newspaper Charlie's brother worked. If she followed the road west out of town, she'd find herself in the neighboring city in fifteen miles or "in no time," Tommy assured her.

Nearly three and a half hours later, somewhat jolted and dusty, Emily reached Cheyenne. She stopped her horse in front of the *Tribune*, where Charlie supposedly worked.

"I hope you are right, Tommy," she murmured as she stepped from the buggy. She brushed her skirt and swiped a hand over her face.

Well, that helped. She had to smile at herself as she removed her gloves, then tried again. Her eyes still felt gritty, but they would do. She tied the horse to the hitching post and entered the newspaper. Oh, my. A large enterprise. It made the *Sun* look like a small-town publication. *And that's just what we are.* No apologies for that.

After she asked for him, it didn't take long for Charlie to appear from the back. He frowned when he saw her. "Ma'am? You want to see me?"

"I am David Martin's sister, Emily." At the mention of her brother's name, Charlie's long thin face drooped farther. But she forged on before he could get in a word. "He's been called away, you know. But he wanted me to publish the *Sun* until he comes home. I can't do that without you. Are you fixed here permanently?"

Her voice didn't sound nearly as forceful as she'd intended. The typesetter stared, eyebrows raised.

"David's coming back? You gonna put out the paper till then?"

She nodded at each question.

"Never heard of a woman doing that." He crossed his arms, his clumps of brown and gray eyebrows lowered, the deep lines at the corners of his eyes shooting into his stringy hair. Charlie obviously didn't like the idea of working for a female.

"I've not had experience with the technical side of the business," she said, pulling on her confident attitude. She hoped it was confident enough. "You would be in charge of that until David returns. I will write the copy and take care of distribution. And, of course, buy supplies."

"So you'll be workin' at the office ever' day?"

His tone of voice didn't sound encouraging either. She nodded once.

He sniffed. "David used to say as how you did a fair bit of writin'. Said you'd be visitin' some this summer."

"And I'm here. Will you come back? Your salary will be the same." She had no idea what that amount was. Lord willing there'd be enough money to pay him.

He uncrossed his arms and stuck his hands in his back pockets. "I'll think on it."

Emily smiled as if he'd already agreed. "Thank you, Charlie. I'm not sure when we can resume printing. The office must be cleaned and the frames repaired, both wood and metal. I'd be very grateful for your help with that too. If you can get away soon."

"If I'm not there by Friday, best look for somebody else." He cleared his throat, started to turn away, then stopped. "What's your view on drinkin' coffee and chewin'?"

"I couldn't work without my tea," she said. "Just as long as it's kept away from the paper and press. Chewing..." She couldn't repress a shiver. "Not in the office. I'm sorry. Will that be a problem?"

"I'll think on it."

His deadpan expression gave no hint of his thoughts, but she feared the No Chewing policy was a deal-killer. She couldn't help it. The thought of a spittoon made her gag. But if that made the difference between Charlie's coming back or not, could she adjust? She didn't know.

She walked across the street to a café for lunch. Just like breakfast, no tea was available, so she ordered coffee to accompany her roast beef and boiled potatoes. A heavier midday meal than she was accustomed to, but the food tasted quite good. Turning down the pie for dessert, she was surprised when the very young waitress insisted, "It comes with the meal. Might as well eat it."

"Perhaps someone else would like it," Emily said.

The girl unexpectedly grinned. "Yes, ma'am. 'Spect they would. I'm partial to cook's apple pie. Thanks."

Another long drive back loomed. She checked her bodice watch. Perhaps she'd time to shop a bit, and Cheyenne Mercantile beckoned on the corner. Tea. Yes. Sometime later, she returned to the buggy, her arms loaded with packages. Tea—honest to goodness tea, a kettle for heating water, a box of stationery, pens and pencils, and a bag of pastries from The Bake Shoppe.

She stowed the purchases on the buggy's floorboard, then set out. She stopped at the livery to water the horse. By the time she tooled out of Cheyenne on the road to Wylder, her watch read two o'clock. Plenty of time to make it home before dark.

Chapter 9

The afternoon breeze fell flat against Morgan's face. It gave no welcome relief, no joy, no comfort. Had a stream flowed near, he would have dived in, clothing and all. The meeting had left him with a sticky feeling that seeped beneath his skin. His past held a dictionary full of run-ins with all kinds of folks, but never one like this.

His first solo job for Foster. Tell the Gordon family their stolen stock hadn't been recovered. He'd carried similar messages before, but none had led to the wife fainting dead away and the young son turning white then losing his breakfast. Gordon—hell, Gordon must have shrunk two inches before his eyes.

Finally he'd muttered, "We're finished, then." He'd looked at Morgan and nodded. "Tell your boss I said thanks for searching."

The daughter—maybe twelve or so with the still-flat figure of a youngster—put her hand on her father's shoulder. "Sit down now, Pa. I'll look to Ma. We'll be fine, you'll see."

Gordon didn't sit, just stood, body tight together, shoulders slumped, arms folded around his chest. The girl knelt beside her mother, who had recovered enough to sit, and used the hem of her dress to blot the blood from a gash on her forehead. The woman began to cry. Not silent tears, but stomach-wrenching sobs of despair.

Morgan shifted in the saddle. The sound of those sobs brought back memories—too many to count. He'd grown weary of hearing them. More than weary—appalled, ashamed of himself, even when he hadn't been the one to cause the devastation.

Those sobs reminded him of why he was finished with this life, yet here he was once more. Hell, he hadn't even had the courtesy to dismount before delivering the crushing news. Gordon glanced toward his wife.

"You been hit before?" Morgan asked.

Gordon nodded. "Twice now. First time, the cattle; this time the cattle and the horses, even the milk cow. Sow was shot. Lost her litter. "

A handful of chickens pecked hopefully at the bare ground. The man nudged one absently and sent it off squawking and flapping. "Not long after the spring wheat came in, a hole in the barn roof opened, and the rain we been waiting for all spring finally come. Wheat molded."

"Pa," the girl said, her voice conciliating, almost pleading, "if'n we sell, we can go back to Illinois. Use the money to buy a place there. Maybe near Grandad."

Gordon didn't answer, just looked at Morgan. "Appreciate the long ride out here." He glanced at his still-sobbing wife. "You might want to head back now."

Morgan nodded. "I'm sorry."

And damned if he wasn't. The Gordon family had managed to touch something deep inside him. He didn't know what to make of his reactions. This whole Wyoming job felt different. He felt different.

His thoughts chased each other in a circle as he rode. Something Gordon had said bothered him, but he couldn't pin it down. Ahead, the trail intersected the road to Wylder. Might not be usual, or advisable, but he decided to ride into town to have a word with Eli Foster.

High puffs of dust came into sight as he neared the turnoff. Looked like a buggy heading for Wylder, its wheels aggravating the dried ground of naked ruts carved by years of wagon and stage travel. The horse pulling the buggy jogged along the flatter verge between the ruts, unconcerned about every rock and hole that sent the driver bouncing.

A particularly deep hole in one rut tipped the equipage. The driver slid sideways against the seat rail, and several packages sailed out onto the ground. The buggy jolted upright again, and the driver pulled the horse to a halt.

She sat for a moment, head bent, shoulders moving as she gulped breath.

She?

What idiot female would be traveling alone on such a road? Must have come from Cheyenne by the looks of the merchandise scattered in the dirt. Well. He couldn't leave her sitting by herself like that. Morgan urged Brag into a canter. In just a few feet, he recognized the driver.

The lady from the train.

What in the fires of holy hell was this Easterner doing out here? Alone. Driving a flimsy buggy. Didn't she have a lick of sense?

He ought to just leave her there. But then the sound of a cry tore at his conscience. Until he deciphered the words in the cry. The lady knew how to swear. That did it. How could he pass her by now? Smothering a laugh he urged Brag on.

"You all right?" Morgan called, making sure no trace of laughter remained in his voice. He reached the buggy and dismounted, dropping his reins to the ground. Brag stood in place. Morgan walked back to gather up the spilled merchandise.

"Yes," she managed, "thank you." She glanced up when he placed the items on the floorboard. Her look of gratitude snapped into recognition. "You. How did you come to be here?"

The side of Morgan's mouth twitched. No tears, no swooning, no falling on his shoulders in gratitude. He might have expected this independence from what he'd seen of her before.

He nodded. "Ma'am. You're welcome."

Sparks danced in her eyes, bloodshot from the dust. "You have a way of doing that."

Her lively tone told Morgan she was, indeed, unhurt. "Ma'am?"

"Catching me unaware and answering before I can even thank you." She stood, wobbling for a moment until she gained her equilibrium. "And please stop 'Ma'am-ing' me. It makes me feel like my grandmother."

"It's a sign of respect where I'm from."

"Yes. Well. Thank you. I…" She gasped as Morgan curled his fingers around her waist. "Put me down."

He swung her from where she stood and set her on firm ground. "Faster and easier this way. You sure you're all right? That last bump grabbed you good."

She absently rubbed the side of her hip where it had hit the metal bar of the buggy seat. "My skirts took most of the blow, I believe. Thank you. I don't remember the road being this rough earlier today."

"Wheel likely hit a hole wrong this time. I'm headed for Wylder myself. I'll tie my horse on back and drive." She raised her chin but before she could refuse he added, "If that's agreeable to you? Doesn't hurt to have an extra pair of hands along on these trips."

Without waiting for an answer, he grabbed Brag's reins and led him around to the rear of the buggy. The lady was applying a handkerchief to her eyes when he returned. Poor lady. Of course her nerves had taken over. Even someone with her determination would be moved to shed a few tears. He gripped her shoulders lightly. "Things'll be fine, now. You're safe, and no harm done. No need for tears."

"I'm not crying." She removed the handkerchief and turned to get into the buggy, muttering, "Why do men think females weep with every breath. I had something in my eyes—dirt, I expect."

Good thing her back was turned, he'd hate for her to see him smile. She'd likely wallop him with her flimsy bag. "That's likely. Plenty of it kicking up today. If you'll scoot over—give me a little room."

She settled herself, careful not to step on the items on the floorboard, and looked ahead. Solemnly she added, "I never cry."

"Yes, ma'am." He enjoyed the way she stiffened and glanced at him. Her spirit looked revived. He smiled, stepped up, and slid onto the seat. For a while, they rode in silence until he became aware of her cutting him occasional glances from beneath lowered eyelids.

Maybe she was a bit shy after all. She was a fine-looking woman, even covered in a thin film of dust. Her shirt must have started the day white, but it shown with a fine gray grit now. All the bouncing had dislodged the pretty little hat, so it sagged over her left eye, and its dandy blue ribbons on the side had jostled loose and mingled in her now-straggling hair.

The sight triggered a wave of warmth that made him shrug. He had to admire her gumption. Even experienced ranch women he'd known didn't venture out on an unfamiliar road without a rifle and a sidearm. And most took along at least one ranch hand, just in case. Again, he wondered who she was.

Finally he said, "If I can't call you ma'am, what can I call you?"

She cleared her throat. A moment later she said, "My name is Emily Martin."

"Glad to meet you, Miss Martin. I'm Morgan Dodd. Just went to work for Eli Foster at the Union Pacific. At his ranch."

She nodded, a cautiously friendly expression. "Is that why you were on the train?"

"That's right." He didn't push for details about her presence in Wylder, but he hoped she'd take his hint.

Finally she did. "I came to visit my brother, but he's been called away. I've been trying to gather equipment I need while I wait for him."

"I saw a kettle and what looked like tea leaves scattered in the dirt back there. Opening a business?"

She snapped her head toward him. "The tea leaves were lost? Oh dear." She sighed. "Well, perhaps the Mercantile in Wylder sells tea. The equipment is for the house. I do like a cup of tea to relax after a long day of work."

"You plan to work here?"

"My brother, David, publishes the newspaper. I had planned to help him for a few weeks."

"But he's out of town? Who's taking care of it now?"

"That's why I went to Cheyenne. When David left, the typesetter took a position at the *Leader* in Cheyenne. He's coming back to the *Sun,* however." Then she murmured, "I'm sure he will."

Morgan almost missed that last comment. "What if he doesn't?"

When Miss Martin didn't answer, he glanced at her profile. Her teeth gripped her lower lip, and lines creased her forehead. Finally she said, "I'll manage somehow."

The frown disappeared and she brushed at her skirt, sending up a small cloud of dust. "But I'm sure Charlie will return. Tomorrow I'll begin to get the office in shape, so we'll have everything ready when he does."

Morgan bit back a smile. Women and their everlasting cleaning. "Needs a little sprucing up, does it?"

"If you haven't been in town since the last time we met, you probably are unaware. The *Sun* office was ransacked, and the press damaged after my brother left town." Her tone sounded oddly strained, as if she tried not to show the strong emotion she likely felt.

"I didn't know," he said. "Sorry to hear it. You got help to fix things?"

"Oh, I'm certain there'll be no problem. The biggest chore will be picking up all the papers strewn around. Sorting all the letters and getting them back in their trays. Once the trays are repaired. I have to find someone to straighten the metal frames and replace the wooden sides."

"Sounds like whoever ransacked the place intended to shut it down." Morgan managed to keep his voice as conversational as hers. Nothing to be gained by ranting and raving about the destruction. She certainly appeared matter of fact about it.

He liked that about her. He liked that about her *also*.

"Maybe," he said, as his mind sifted through options, "the blacksmith could straighten any metal for you. Don't know if there's a carpenter shop for the frame, but the bakery lady could tell you that."

She turned to him abruptly. "That's a splendid idea. I'll visit the blacksmith tomorrow. And perhaps Tommy at the livery can suggest some boys to help with the general clean up. Thank you."

He glanced her way, and she smiled. A real smile, not a pleasant twist of the lips. It sent a sharp jolt to his chest, and he inhaled. Damn, she was pretty. Dirt-streaked face, scraggly hair, dusty clothes, and all. But that smile made him feel like he'd done something special, like score a half-dozen bull's eyes in a row to win the grand prize heifer or ride a wild bronc to a stand-still when all others had failed. He squared his shoulders and flicked the reins.

He thought she might explain further, but after a sigh, she swiveled to face forward again.

They rode in silence for a while until she said, "The country here is beautiful. Such a different feel from the countryside at home."

"Where's home?" He guessed Chicago, maybe even farther east.

"Missouri—"

He jerked upright. Missouri? A cold chill settled over him despite the heat. What the hell were the odds... "Where—"

"Kansas City is where I grew up, although my grandparents live several miles from there on a farm."

"Which direction?" He tried to keep his voice level. No use alarming her.

"Let's see—east. Near Jefferson City."

Relief was a sweet, slow exhale. Far enough, then.

"My uncle runs the place now. I always love visiting there. But the space here just seems—different, somehow."

He had no answer for that. His mind lingered on his apprehension. After all these years, why did the memory still seem so fresh?

He cleared his throat. "So, your folks don't farm?"

Miss Martin chuckled. "Father always said he could never figure out a planting schedule. But he can certainly figure out a court docket. He's a lawyer."

That explained a lot about the lady seated beside him. Her way of speaking, even her way of moving. She'd been raised to circulate in society. He cut her a glance. Why hadn't a woman like her married long before now?

He considered asking that question when the horse clopped around a curve and ahead lay Wylder. It stretched out before him like nearly every other frontier town he'd passed through. Bigger than some, smaller than others. Streets running straight. Buildings hunched together, their different sizes like jagged teeth against the sky.

Odd that he felt different about this place as the

tired horse pulled the rig nearer. Although he'd spent only a few hours in the various businesses when he first arrived, the town carried a kind of draw. Familiar, maybe? Like coming home, maybe? *God, no! Never like going home.*

Far behind the orderly laid out streets and neat buildings loomed the mountains. That must be what felt inviting. Just over those peaks lay his new beginning.

Miss Martin remained silent until they approached the edge of town.

"The house is on the street behind the newspaper," she said. "There."

When the buggy stopped, he got out and rounded the back to give her a hand.

"I appreciate your help, Mr. Dodd. Good luck in your new job."

He touched the brim of his hat. "Miss Martin. I wish you good fortune with your brother's newspaper. And ma'am, think about taking someone along next time you drive out. No telling what danger a lady alone might run on to."

He untied Brag, mounted, and started toward town and the depot. *No looking back.* But the memories of their talk stayed with him until he reached the Union Pacific offices. Foster stood outside, eyes squinted grimly, hands on hips.

"Damn it, Dodd, can't you do a simple job right?"

Chapter 10

What the hell has the boss in a tizzy? Morgan met Foster's gaze as he swung from the saddle, and the agent gave a jerk of his head toward the office. Stifling heat hit Morgan in the face when he stepped inside. The door banged shut, and he drew in a lungful of heavy air.

"Damned if this isn't the hottest July I can remember out here," Foster grumbled, distracted for a moment from his earlier rant. He grabbed a handkerchief from the desk drawer and swiped it across his face.

"Nice breeze outside. Open a window?" Morgan took a step toward one, but Foster threw up a hand.

"Can't open the damned things. Dirt blows in, flies and gnats everywhere." He plopped into his chair then fished a paper from a wire basket on the desktop and fanned himself with it. "Explain yourself. You're supposed to be working, not escorting the new woman around. You had a job to do—notifying the Gordons they're done up."

Morgan folded onto one of the chairs nearby and dropped his hat onto the seat of another. He propped his right ankle on the opposite knee, blotted drops of perspiration from his forehead with a forearm, then leaned back. He seemed relaxed, most folks would think. Most folks would be wrong.

He had no idea what Foster meant, and the man's

truculent expression gave him no clue. "Not sure what you're talking about. I just got back from giving Gordon the news about his stock. Wife took it pretty hard. The daughter argued to sell out and go back home. He might just do that. He looked…broken."

Foster met Morgan's gaze, his own blank of any emotion Morgan could read. "You talked to him, then?"

"Those were the orders. What gave you the idea I didn't carry them out?"

"Ray and the boys were on the way back when they saw you driving Miss Martin on the road from Cheyenne. That's not the road to the ranch."

Morgan took a moment to calm the anger pulsing higher with every word from the agent. "Doesn't seem like the boys were headed to the ranch themselves if they crossed the Cheyenne road. Were they out checking on me?"

Something in his tone must have hit Foster because he stopped fanning, paper suspended in air. "Nobody's checking up on you. They had their own assignment, then took the railroad trail into town—shorter, but it's got a view of the other road. Ray thought I should know. He's a good foreman."

"Mighty kind of him." Morgan swung his foot to the floor and sat forward. "As a matter of fact, I was on my way to talk to you myself. I got the impression the Gordons'll be ready to talk sale in a day or so. Thought maybe you'd be interested in a nice right-of-way section coming open, before the word gets around to anyone else."

Foster stared at him for a full ten seconds— Morgan counted—before his mouth lost its downturned line and curved up. His eyes crinkled at the corners, their expression finally showing his thoughts. Greed and...smugness.

"You're right. Good thinking." He resumed fanning.

Morgan braced his forearms on his knees. "I ran into Miss Martin on the road, having a little trouble with her rig. Wouldn't be gentlemanly to leave her stranded."

Foster chuckled. "No, it wouldn't, would it? Good, good. I want her to know my men are courteous." He dug around in a stack of papers until he pulled out a Wanted flyer. "I haven't explained about the first job I told you about. You might've guessed some of it after today."

He handed over the flyer. "We've had a mighty lot of rustling going on around Wylder these past months. Big ranchers and small, they've all been hit. The sheriff has so much to tend to, I've offered to let my crew help out. We follow the outlaws' trails, take back the stock, and return it to the owners. Sometimes our efforts fail, like they did with the Gordons' cattle. Many of those small spreads can't stand the loss. I hate to see folks suffer for our failures, so when I can I buy 'em up if they're wanting to sell.

"That," he nodded to the paper Morgan held, "is one of the rustlers we're looking for. His gang took more than seventy-five head of prime cattle from the Tall T, Joe Trimble's ranch. It's located northeast of here. I'll see you get directions."

Morgan examined the hand-drawn features represented in the picture. Not much chance of recognizing anyone from it, but it might come in handy. He stood, folded the paper, and slid it into his back pocket.

"One thing about this theft," Foster said. "We usually find the cattle not many miles away, but this lot—no trace of them until a couple of days ago. Trimble got word his brand was recognized on a couple cows up in Laramie. One of my own turned up in Cheyenne. I want you to find the rest of Trimble's cattle and bring back the thief. Better yet, dispose of him. Just bring back the cattle."

"Sounds like this particular theft is important to you. You just said some were found, some not. What's different about this one?"

Foster's glance pinned Morgan, sharp as the darning needle his mother had used. "Your business is to follow orders. Not ask questions. God knows, I'm paying you enough for the pleasure of your gun's company. But just this once, I'll tell you. Trimble's got a hell of a lot of friends around here. Not only that, he's an important man in Wyoming with important connections back East. I can't afford to let him down.

"The last crew I sent after this robber spent two months on the trail and got nowhere. I'm trusting you to see the job done."

Morgan nodded. "I'll set out tomorrow early."

"Take whatever men you need."

"I work alone." He picked up his hat, gestured goodbye with it, then paused at the door. "By the way. Thought I'd get a drink. What place do the boys favor?"

Ten minutes later, he tied Brag outside the Longhorn Saloon, shook out his hands, and loosened his shoulders. He stepped up on the boardwalk and pushed through the door. Along the bar to the left stood the crew from the Bar F. None of them noticed his approach. Ray was talking to the cowboy on his right when Morgan shouldered in on the other side, leaned on his forearms, and signaled the barkeep for a drink.

"Ray." His voice was low, but its deep timbre carried through the noise. Ray looked up.

"What'd ya want?" The foreman finished his drink and spun the glass to the side along the bar's scarred wooden surface.

Morgan turned on his left elbow, his right arm coming to rest at his side, leaving his hand free and near his gun.

"What I do on my own time is my concern." His voice was soft, his tone conversational, but the words strung out on a steel thread. "What I do on the job is the boss's. None of it is yours. No more spying."

Ray bristled. "You report to me. I'm foreman. The boss sent you out on a job and next time I see you, you're riding along, cozying up to some fancy lady."

Morgan straightened and faced the other man. "I reported to the boss. But I'll tell you this once. I did the notification. Until there's another job for me, my time's my own. Keep your nose out of my business."

A flicker of challenge lit the foreman's eyes as the man faced Morgan. "Or what?" he mocked. "You gonna shoot me dead?" He snorted. "I ain't impressed with you. I ain't seen nothing yet that makes me believe one half of them tales the boss likes to tell. Me, I think the rumors are bigger than you are. Probably told 'em all yourself."

Some of the crew had become aware of the confrontation and watched maliciously. At Ray's jibe, they snickered.

Morgan's right palm began to itch, his fingers

tingle. He studied the foreman and the three along the bar beside him. They all were likely up a few drinks and looking to have their boredom relieved. And Ray? Morgan judged the man considered himself Big Dog around here and was busy marking his territory.

Morgan wasn't in the habit of interfering in territories. He'd move on soon, and Ray'd be welcome to howl all he wanted.

As for fighting for bragging rights? No sense to it. That happened only once, years ago. He got his trusted Brag out of that quarrel, but it wouldn't happen again. Nope. He was here for the money. All he had to do was remember California and that peaceful life he wanted.

Recalling his plans held Morgan quiet long enough for Ray to figure he'd made his point. He chuckled and turned back, signaling for another drink.

Morgan's eased straight, his hand anticipating the feel of his gun. And out of nowhere flashed a similar scene from another town. And another. After all these years, surely he'd learned a bit of wisdom. He felt his mouth twist up in a rueful smile. No sense pushing anything. What did he care about people's opinions? He'd be gone soon. His muscles eased. He lounged back to the bar and picked up his drink. Hell of it was he didn't recall the names of every town along the trails he'd wandered the past dozen years or more.

Job to job, town to town. He was getting weary of it all—had been for a while. Thus this job in Wyoming, where he could launch across the mountains to a new life.

"Just wondering, Dodd." Ray's voice cut into the thoughts. "Who is the fancy lady you was escorting home? Haven't seen her around town before. She new?"

Before Morgan could answer, the cowboy on Ray's right gave a "Ha!" He buffeted Ray on the shoulder. "You don't know who that newcomer is? Why, Ray, I heard that's the editor's sister. Come to visit him and help out at the newspaper."

His words triggered snide laughter along the line of men.

"You don't say." Ray shifted his shoulders and gave a grunt of a laugh. "Po-o-o-or lady. Guess she come a long way for nothing. Reckon we ought to drop around at the paper office and offer to help out?"

His words brought another round of laughter. Morgan wouldn't let them prod him into a fight about the lady, so long as they didn't offer her harm. But if he remained here longer, a confrontation might well get out of hand.

He threw back the rest of his whiskey. "Where's a good eating place?" he asked as he shoved away from the bar.

"Jake's," the bartender said, grabbing up the empty glass. "Just down the street."

Morgan nodded thanks. "See you boys later."

Nobody answered.

Chapter 11

Emily left Dugan's Blacksmith Shop, humming a sprightly waltz. The late afternoon sun shone brightly, capping dust particles in the air with tiny haloes. A cooling breeze ambled down the walkway, teasing fugitive tendrils of hair at her temples and nape. She'd changed her clothes and pinned her hair up beneath a fresh hat after she'd returned from Cheyenne. All in all, the day had been a success. She inhaled until her toes tingled—she hadn't drawn such a deep, satisfying breath since the train left Omaha. She coughed. *No more deep breaths while crossing dirt streets, missy.* Even that didn't stop her smile.

A blacksmith's apprentice promised to stop by in the morning for a look at the damaged plates. And when she returned the horse and buggy to the livery, Tommy had agreed to bring along one of his friends early tomorrow to help straighten up.

Now she intended to stop at the office to make a list of projects for the boys. She paused at the corner and while a rider passed, the odor of frying meat wafted on the breeze. Answering the siren call of food, her stomach rumbled. She pressed a hand against her middle and chuckled.

Perhaps a bite of dinner first. Her bodice watch showed nearly six-fifteen. Not late enough by home standards, but she could set her own rules now. Lifting her hems, she crossed the dirt road, careful to step around a deposit from the horse that had just passed. That odor nearly spoiled her awakening appetite, but as a frequent visitor to her uncle's farm, she had plenty of experience with animal smells.

They simply required getting used to again.

She paused for a couple entering the land office and on the spur of the moment, decided to take what looked like a shortcut to the Vincent House Hotel dining room. But as she crossed between the Catholic Church and the tobacco store, she caught another enticing aroma of the fried—chicken. That was it. And it came from Jake's Place. Her stomach rumbled in earnest. That chicken smelled nearly as good as Bitty made.

Emily swerved to the left and entered the back door of Jake's. The dining room lay straight ahead. At the edge of the seating area, she paused and blinked at the din. Nearly every seat was filled, some with cowboys, several with what appeared to be shopkeepers and their wives, and a few with soldiers who looked bent on enjoying a leave. Every last one must have been shouting.

She didn't see a vacancy and was about to turn when she spied a raised arm. Someone at a small table in the corner. Craning her neck, she identified Morgan Dodd motioning to her.

Did she want to join a stranger? But she did know him. Certainly more than she'd known some men she'd dined with in the past. It took only a moment to decide. As she approached the table, he rose and pulled out the other chair for her.

She drew in a breath to thank him, but when she

caught his gaze, she didn't speak. His expression said it all—commiseration from one friend to another, punctuated by a rueful smile.

Friend? Perhaps so.

The connection she sensed between them put her at ease. She returned his smile and sat. "Thank you. I'm surprised to see so many customers."

He resumed his seat as a waitress arrived carrying a coffee pot and a plate loaded with fried chicken, fried potatoes, green beans, and sliced tomatoes. As she plunked the plate to the table, she refilled his coffee cup.

"Coffee?" she asked, looking at Emily.

"Thank you. And a menu, please, although I'm sure I'll have the chicken. The smell of it cooking lured me in."

The waitress cocked her head to the side. "Ma'am, tonight we got chicken. That's the menu."

Emily looked at Morgan as the waitress left. "I still have a lot to learn about Wylder."

"You and me both." He quirked a brow, then took a drink of coffee. She followed the mesmerizing movement of his throat as he swallowed. How could a simple act be so fascinating?

Clearing her own throat, she rearranged her reticule in her lap. "Did your afternoon go well?"

He held the cup between both hands, his elbows propped on either side of his plate. "Fine. How about yours? I assume you turned in the rig at the livery. Did you find the boy you wanted to talk to?"

"Not only that"—she leaned forward eagerly, wrist on the edge of the table—"Tommy is bringing a friend to help tomorrow morning. Oh, and the blacksmith said he could repair the plates." She paused before adding shyly, "I've had a productive day. Thank you, again, for all your help."

"My pleasure, Miss Martin."

Funny how those simple words made her heart dip. It was the tone of his voice. The slightly rough texture made her think of a caress, of dark nights and confined spaces. Funny, because she'd not experienced either one of those before. Randolph had tried—but when she'd refused, he hadn't asked again. More and more, Emily felt relief when she thought of her former fiancé's ultimatum and her decision.

"Why don't I stop by the *Sun* tomorrow and see if I can—" Morgan was interrupted by the waitress, who returned with Emily's plate of food and cup of coffee. For the next few minutes Emily and Morgan ate in silence. Only once did she throw a covert glance his way—to find him watching her as well. Both jerked their gazes away.

She felt rather than saw a change in his attitude, as if some tension had lessened or wall lowered. The atmosphere seemed easier, more relaxed. She felt drawn to him. Even more than before.

"Miss Martin—" Whatever he intended to say was lost in a shout from the front door.

"Bar F. Meet at the sheriff's."

Emily looked up, but the messenger had disappeared. A pair of cowboys rose from a table on the opposite side of the room and made for the front, slapping on their hats as they went. Morgan made use of his napkin and stood. "Best see what the ruckus is about."

He pulled some change from a pocket, placed it

beside his plate, and turned. He paused and looked down at her. "Supper's on me."

She thought he was about to say something else, but he simply gave a short nod then headed toward the door. The rhythm in his gait, smooth and easy, reminded Emily of the first time she'd seen him, leaping down from the train's stock car. Graceful, contained, yet full of power. And sure enough, a group of entering diners melted aside, leaving a wide path for him.

The waitress returned to refill her coffee cup. "Anything else for you?"

"Thank you, no. The food is delicious. I didn't see a price listed?"

The woman ran a finger over the coins beside the empty plate. "Never mind. All took care of." She glanced up. "Hope to see you back in, Miss Martin."

Surprised at the use of her name, Emily was about to reply when a voice from a nearby table had the waitress wheeling away. Small towns were the same everywhere, evidently. Newcomers didn't stay strangers for long.

****

Morgan stopped at the edge of the men congregated in the street outside the sheriff's office. Foster stood beside the solid figure of Sheriff Hanson in front of the door. The sheriff's tidy gray moustache drooped around a firm mouth and resolute chin. Finally, when no more stragglers joined the crowd, he spoke.

"Men, rustlers struck again, but it's a different story this time. They hit the Circle O late last night. Shot Sven Olsen. Doc just got back—Sven died this afternoon."

Morgan hadn't heard of the Olsens, but from the murmurs and curses that rose at the news, this Sven must have been well thought of. Willie sidled up on the left.

"Damn," he muttered, words slurred. "Hate to hear that. Old Sven was okay. He'd 'a probably give 'em the damn cows if they'd 'ast. He was like that. Give up his longjohns in winter if a man needed 'em."

The sheriff's voice rose over the din. "Don't have to tell you what this means, now they've gone from stealing stock to murder."

"We'll help you find them," Foster called out, "won't we men?"

The Bar F hands echoed his shout.

The sheriff raised his hand for quiet. "I'll take a posse southeast, out to the Circle O and start from there."

Foster nodded. "My men will head north. I'll send a runner to your office here with any news." He strode to the end of the walk. "Bar F, meet at my office with your mounts in half an hour. Ray, Dodd, I want to talk to you."

Morgan ambled to where Foster stood. Ray stumbled up, straight from the Longhorn judging by the fumes surrounding him. His eyes were bloodshot, but steady, cold.

Foster folded his arms. "I don't care what beef you two got with each other. Put it behind you while you're working, understood?"

How the hell did Foster know about the spat at the Longhorn?

"I got a feeling about this one," he went on. "Ray, I expect you know what I'm thinking."

Ray flicked his hat back a notch on his forehead. "Snake Rocks is a good place to fix brands. Circle O could be a Bullseye in no time. Would he dare, so close?"

"I warned him last time." Foster's voice fell hard, and Morgan detected an undercurrent to the words. His suspicion was confirmed when Ray gave a short nod and pulled the brim of his hat down to his forehead again.

Foster knew who the rustlers were. And from the sound of it, well…Morgan would have to do a little digging to see if that hunch was right.

"Ray, take Dodd with you. Dodd, a word first."

Morgan moved closer as Ray headed down the street toward the livery. Foster stepped from the walk onto the ground and lowered his voice. "I got a good idea who's behind this. Same one on that Wanted poster I showed you. Calls himself Bob Roberts now. The man used to work for me but took the notion to go it on his own. He's got no spread, but he's claimed a brand. The Bullseye. When he rode for me he was called Bobby Bullseye."

Morgan snorted.

"Yeah, well, out here folks can pretty much be who they want to. Don't usually matter. Except when they get their stock from everybody around—without paying. This time, Bobby's gone too far. He can't be allowed to keep it up. Thing is, he don't need to be brought all the way back to town to face a noose."

"But if he surrenders—"

"He *won't*." Foster gave him a level stare, his mouth narrowed into a tight line. Then he raised his eyebrows. "He won't, will he?"

Morgan understood, all right. This Bobby Bullseye must know something Foster didn't want shared with the town. Suddenly, his mind snapped back to the name Bullseye...Bob...Bobby Bullseye.

Holy hell. It couldn't be. He'd once known a Bobby, nicknamed Bullseye because of his shooting power. Couple years older than Morgan'd been at fourteen—a rowdy and boastful youth, the pride of the nearby Bushwhackers. Couldn't be the same man.

But maybe it could. Before he'd deserted what was left of home, Morgan had heard Bobby joined a group up around St. Joe. Memories of those days roiled through him like the grippe, leaving him hot, then cold, then so sick he nearly gagged. More than thirteen years since they'd seen each other. Likely he'd changed enough that Bobby wouldn't recognize him. Morgan'd been a skinny, scared kid then.

Foster's voice broke through the fog of memory. "If you, Ray, and the boys don't come up on him and the cattle tonight, I want you to go on to Cheyenne, see what you can find there. If you must, follow him to Laramie. Just find the son of a bitch. Questions?"

Morgan thought for a moment. "Anything more you can tell me about him?"

After a pause when it seemed like he had something else to say, Foster eventually shook his head. "Not that'll make any difference to your search. Just know he's got it in for me. He's likely hoping to make me chase him down myself. But I won't give him that satisfaction. Besides"—he cocked his head in an unconscious preen—"if I'm to move into politics, I don't need a shooting to haunt me."

"Politics, huh?" It was a chancy question, but the

boss cast a possessive look around.

"Wylder doesn't have a mayor, did you know? Special election coming up, and I intend to run."

"And win?"

Foster chuckled, a distant look in his eyes. "I don't lose."

"But don't mayors have to live in the town?"

"Not for you to worry about. It's taken care of. Now, go catch up with Ray—and Dodd, don't rile him. I don't want to lose either of you just yet."

Chapter 12

After a quick breakfast of stale tea and a pastry that barely escaped a dirt bath yesterday on the return from Cheyenne, Emily tended to kitty, then walked to the newspaper office. She was happy to see Tommy and another boy arriving at the same time.

"Good morning, gentlemen."

"Morning, ma'am," Tommy replied. He motioned to his friend. "This is Joey. He's gonna help today."

"Happy to meet you, Joey." As she unlocked the door, a stomach rumbled behind her. Hadn't they eaten?

"Have you gentlemen had breakfast yet?" she asked, stepping inside and propping the door open with a brick that looked like it usually served that purpose.

"No ma'am," Tommy said. "I mostly don't eat nothing afore lunch."

Joey merely looked around at the mess on the floor and shook his head.

Boys that age needed food. And Emily feared neither had access to it at home, wherever that might be. She'd ask Tommy. Later. She wasn't hungry, but the boys were so thin, so eager to help. She couldn't resist.

"You know, I left home quickly this morning too. Why don't you run over to the hotel and ask if they have some breakfast biscuits. And milk. You need milk."

"Milk," Joey scoffed. "I ain't no baby."

Tommy snickered, but when Emily glanced at him, his cheeks reddened, and he hushed.

"Then get what you'd like to drink. Here." She opened her reticule and handed some coins to Tommy. "Tell them we'll return the dishes later."

When the two left she pulled a sheet of paper from her reticule and reviewed the tasks she'd listed last night. By the time the boys returned, she'd sketched a plan for the day's jobs.

Tommy and Joey each carried a tray, one loaded with fragrant hot biscuits and dishes of butter and jam, the other with cups of steaming coffee and knifes and spoons. They slid the trays on the front desk and served themselves.

Before Tommy bit into his biscuit, he looked at her guiltily. "Ma'am, you want one?"

"You two go ahead. I'll be there in a moment." She wrestled the last bundle of record *Sun*s onto the bottom level of the large, wooden shelves that divided the front of the office from the back on one side. Thank goodness those files hadn't been destroyed. Most newspapers kept a copy of each issue as an official record of publication. Many offices stored each year's issues of record in separate stacks, pressed between thick cardboard covers. They reminded Emily of giant books, stacked flat on the shelves.

The Wylder Sun had been established in 1869, David had said, the same year as the town, so there should be nine large cardboard "books." After accounting for all nine, Emily went to the desk.

A lone biscuit awaited her, centered in the plate, a coffee cup at its edge. The boys had been starved, from the looks of it.

"We saved you one, Miss Emily," Tommy said, somewhat apologetically.

"Thank you." Seeing the large size of the biscuit, she judged the hotel had sent a half dozen. Which meant the boys should be stuffed. Yet they gazed longingly at the tray. "It looks delicious, but you know, that coffee is about all I want this early in the day. Why don't you two share it?"

Joey propped his elbows on the desk and looked at Tommy. Finally, Tommy said, "'S all right, ma'am. We each had one. That 'un's yours."

She smiled. "You could have brought more, you know."

"Well, um," Tommy flashed Joey a look. "The hotel sent six, but we saw Jamie Gordon ridin' in to get the doc. His ma's not doin' so good, and he hadn't ate yet. So we give him one for hisself, and one for his pa and sis, to take home."

Emily's throat tightened. What a thoughtful gesture from these two hungry boys. "That was very kind of you. Did he say what was wrong with the mother?"

"She went all to pieces, like, 'cause they gotta move," piped up Joey.

"Rustlers hit their place a few days ago. Took their stock and burned the barn," Tommy explained. "Mr. Foster had men out lookin', but Jamie's pa found out yesterday the cattle were gone for good."

Yesterday? If Eli Foster's men hadn't been able to find the animals, then Morgan Dodd must have notified the Gordons yesterday. He said he'd been delivering some kind of news. "Is the Gordons' place east of here?"

Tommy nodded.

So that's what'd had him looking grim. "I'm so sorry. I wonder if there's anything I can do?"

"Reckon word'll be coming if they need help," Tommy said. "Happens sometimes."

Perhaps she could ask someone later—Cissy at the bakery?

"Go ahead, now." She nodded toward the plate. "We don't want that to go to waste."

She didn't have to offer twice.

Energized by their food, the boys set to work. They gathered all the papers from the floor, straightened them, then stacked them on the desk for Emily to look over. Any that seemed important she placed in a drawer, the others she discarded in a small keg. When the keg was filled, one of the youths took it out back to what they called the burn pile, an area inside a circle of rocks apparently used for burning trash.

They had set fire to the first load before Emily realized what they were doing. When she smelled smoke, she leapt to her feet to investigate, calling out, "Fire." That made the boys laugh so hard they had to sit down. Finally, they explained how burnables were disposed of in Wylder.

"Most ever' house has a burn pile out back," Tommy finally stopped giggling long enough to say. "It's no big thing to worry about. I tend ours at the livery all the time."

Emily finally smiled at her alarm, chalking up the experience to one more thing she had to learn about her new life. "All right," she said, "but one of you keep a watch on that fire. It's terribly dangerous."

"Yes, ma'am," Joey said. "But there's no wind so

we oughta be fine."

Faster than she thought possible, the papers were off the floor, the books restored to the bookshelves, and the splintered wood that had been a chair and a small desk had been stacked behind the office to be disposed of or used as kindling.

Emily's watch showed nearly eleven-thirty.

"We've made wonderful time," she said as they surveyed the finally uncluttered reception area. "Let's take time for lunch now and start on the back this afternoon."

That reminded her that the smithy's apprentice hadn't stopped by as he'd promised. Perhaps he'd make it in later. "Let's wash up, and we'll eat at the hotel." About mid-morning, Tommy had fetched a pail of water from a nearby well for drinking. They could use the basin in the sleeping quarters in back for washing.

Tommy stopped cold. "Us too? Really? You'll buy our lunch?"

"Well, of course. I employed you for the day, and food was included." She glanced at Joey. "Is that all right with you?"

She'd meant the question as an offhand reassurance, but the youth took her seriously.

Turning mournful eyes on her, he said, "I always wanted to eat at Jake's Place. Can we go there instead?"

She chuckled. "I suppose it doesn't matter. Tommy, will that work for you?"

He answered with a big smile.

Emily had never been around youngsters much, especially ones in their teen years. But she found she got along well with the two boys—or young men. Perhaps because they were a bit uncertain around her, as well. As lunch concluded and the afternoon passed, the three developed an easy relationship.

The clean up of the working area and press quarters went quickly, considering the printer's drawers for the individual letters had yet to be repaired. Emily had Tommy and Joey arrange the metal alphabet letters in order on the worktable, to be loaded when the wooden slots were ready.

By five o'clock, all the debris had been cleared, letters separated on the table, wooden trays stacked for repair, and the press pieces carefully placed around the remaining intact machine. All that remained was a good dusting and scrubbing. Emily would see to that tomorrow.

Before her workers scurried off, she bid them come to the front. There, she laid out a paper dollar for each boy. "Thank you for your hard work today, gentlemen."

"Go-o-l-l," the two whispered at the same time, staring at their payment, eyes round as silver dollars. Perhaps they would have preferred coins? She wasn't sure which form of currency was best here.

"Miss Emily," Tommy said—she'd become Miss Emily sometime during the afternoon—"this is an awful lot of money. You sure you didn't mistake it?"

"You earned every bit of your pay. I've never seen young men work so hard all day as you have. But if you'd prefer to have payment in coins, there's time to have this changed at the bank."

"Oh no, ma'am," Tommy said. "But we don't feel right, takin' all this. We'll come back and help out again, won't we Joey?"

His friend, still enthralled by the bill he held, simply nodded.

"I have to work at the livery tomorrow, but later in the week, if'n that'll be okay?"

Emily smiled and patted him on the shoulder. "Whatever you like, Tommy. I will always be happy to have you here. And you, too, Joey."

Alone again, she sank into the chair behind the front desk. Despite the progress made today, so much remained to be done before a paper could ever be published. She shot upright in the chair. Paper. Oh goodness, she'd not even thought of that. Where did David keep the blank pages for printing? Certainly not here in the office. And if there was none, where could she get a new supply?

Chapter 13

The boys had been gone nearly an hour when Emily tipped her head back and closed her stinging eyes. The list of repairs and supplies filled an entire sheet of paper, and the obstacles seemed endless. But she couldn't allow that thought to extinguish her usual optimism. Nothing was so bad it couldn't be fixed.

Yet no matter what she did, more problems kept bobbing up. Perhaps she wasn't meant to carry on with this newspaper idea. Why had she ever thought she could?

"Hello?"

Emily yelped at the unexpected voice. She swung around, her still-blurry vision smudging the identity of the man standing at the front door. But she recognized the warm, rough tones. Blinking rapidly, she brought Morgan into clarity.

"Didn't mean to startle you." He ambled toward the desk and removed his hat.

"I thought you were gone," she said. Then, "I'm sorry. That sounded unwelcoming. Would you like to sit?"

He shook his head. "Saw the open door when I rode past, thought I'd see how clean up went."

Emily's heart still pounded. She took a couple of deep breaths. She wasn't at all sure her pulse raced from surprise only. "I hadn't expected to see you so soon. The word last night after you left was that the men were on the trail of cattle thieves."

"We found the cattle." Leaning a hip against a corner of the desk, he folded his arms across his chest and stared at the street. "At least, most."

"That's good, isn't it?" Capturing the outlaws and finding the stock was exactly what they set out to do. Except, Morgan didn't look satisfied. In fact, he looked restless, almost haunted. She murmured, "What's wrong?"

"The men escaped," he said, finally. "Don't know how that happened. Looked like they were pinned down, but when we stormed the hiding place, they'd disappeared. After we'd followed them all night, none of the boys wanted to go any farther. We got the cattle, though. Drove them back to the Olsen ranch and came to town to report."

"Perhaps the sheriff has some ideas," she said.

He looked down, his eyes losing their glazed, far-away expression and focusing on her. "Maybe. Hope he does. But things didn't seem right."

Emily fought an urge to smooth away his lingering frown, ease the lines of exhaustion around his eyes. "You haven't slept since I saw you last, have you? You must be ready to drop."

"I'm fine." He straightened. "What did you get done today? Did your helper show up?"

"He did." She rose, ridiculously happy he wanted to stay. She welcomed his company. Perhaps a little too much. "He brought a friend, and we managed to clear away the debris. I'll show you."

She led him around the office, pointing out some of the projects that had been accomplished. When they arrived at the back where the pieces of press lay grouped and the metal letters spread across a table, he let out a low whistle.

"Quite a sorry sight. Looks like you need a new machine."

"I think it's just disassembled—I mean it's in pieces, but it's an old model, and the metal parts are heavy. Most of this can be put back together pretty quickly—if someone knew how to do it."

"You don't?" He knelt beside the base where it was attached to the floor.

"I'm afraid not. There—the platform that holds the frame for letters has been damaged. That's what I hoped the blacksmith could fix."

Morgan stood. "So it's not as bad as it looks?"

"I don't believe so. If Charlie comes back and if the blacksmith can straighten the plates, we should be able to print again. If we find the paper." Another thought hit her. "Oh, no. Ink." She turned to him. "I don't know about the ink."

The whole day collapsed around her just then, and her knees turned to jelly. Wonderful. All she needed was to melt into a blob at his feet. She whispered, "I think I'll sit down."

She must have bobbled because the next thing she knew, he'd slid one arm around her shoulders and another around her waist. "Steady. You're just tired."

Instinctively, she clung to him. His arms tightened, and she looked up. His face, shadowed by the brim of his hat, was a mysterious plane, and his dark gaze seemed to swallow her. Her breath stopped somewhere between her chest and her throat.

She watched in a daze as he gradually lowered his

head.

He's going to kiss me. I should turn away. But she couldn't.

In the seconds it took for his mouth to descend, a hundred thoughts tumbled through her mind. She was scandalous. Shameless. She didn't know him. Yet had she known any of her erstwhile suitors any better the first time they'd ventured a kiss? No. She'd actually spent more time alone with this cowboy…

Her mind stopped at the touch of his lips. Soft, firm, warm. As if a spark flared between them, she jerked her mouth away in surprise, in wonder.

Her head came to rest on his warm, solid chest. Through the fabric of his shirt, his heart pounded against her cheek. Giving a shuddering breath, she ventured a peek upward. His face was set, his mouth a straight line. If she hadn't felt his heart thudding in double time with her own, she'd swear he was untouched by their kiss.

"I…I…" Her voice trembled.

"I'm sorry," he interrupted.

"Don't apologize," she said. "It was mutual."

He caught her gaze, his eyes smoky, intent.

"I'm not sorry I kissed you. I'm sorry I have to leave." He smiled then, the warmth and charm of it wrapping her in its own embrace.

Her face burned when she realized what he'd said.

"Oh." She stepped away. "You…"

He chuckled and drew her back against him. "I have to get to the ranch. The others stopped for a drink at the Longhorn, but they'll be heading out soon."

He kissed her forehead then set her away, running his hands down her arms. When his expression sobered,

Emily guessed his thoughts had gone back to the night's events. He took her elbow as they walked to the front. "Some questions about today need to be answered."

"About the theft?"

"That and other things." He faced her when they reached the desk. "I'll see you soon." He paused, then added, "If you like?"

She smiled. "Yes, please."

A movement at the still-open door made both of them turn.

Ray.

He strode in with a challenging smirk.

"Hey, Dodd, saw your mount outside. Time to be goin'," he said, his voice loud. He advanced to within touching distance of Emily.

She winced at the stench of whiskey, bad breath, and dirty, sweaty male.

"So this is the skirt you been after, huh? Miss Newspaper's Sister?"

Upper lip curled in a snide half smile, he paced into the open area beyond the desk. "Heard your brother had some trouble in here. Looks like you straightened up. Too bad about that thing he prints on, though. Broke apart, I heard. Reckon that comes when you put your nose where it ain't supposed to be. Where'd he go, anyway? Slunk off with his tail between his legs, I reckon."

"You reckon wrong," Emily snapped. "He—"

"You're right, Ray, we better go." Morgan cut in. "The boss wants to talk in the morning and I, for one, need some shut-eye." He started for the door, then stopped. "You coming?"

"Yeah, yeah." Ray swung around, one foot going wide to steady a wobble, the only sign he'd given that he was drunk. He winked at her as he passed. "You be careful, pretty lady."

Morgan waited for Ray to precede him, then glanced at Emily. "I'll see you when I can. And, yeah, be careful."

Emily sank into a chair, elbows on the desk, head buried in her hands. Her mind overflowed with thoughts and images and smells and feelings. A potpourri of emotions.

Not one emerged to the fore. Numb, that's what she felt. And hungry. Some food might raise her spirits.

Should she change before she went to dinner? Thanks to the cloth she'd tied around her waist earlier, her skirt was relatively clean. Perhaps she could manage to look presentable enough for public. Returning to the house for different clothes wasn't feasible. She'd never make it past the bed if she went home first.

How handy it would be to have a change of garments here for times like this. They could be stored in the sleeping area in the back corner. Great idea. Now, however, she rose, took her reticule from a drawer, and headed to the hotel.

****

Morgan and Ray caught up to the rest of the crew in less than half a mile. Ray rode to the head of the group, but Morgan trailed along in back. He had some thoughts to sort out. Not about Miss Martin. Emily. Those thoughts he'd save for later. Right now, he sure as hell would like to know how three, maybe four, men on horseback got away without being seen or heard.

They'd been tracked to Snake Rocks all right. Just where the boss figured they'd go. But no trace could be found of anyone vaguely resembling a leader like Bobby Bullseye.

Willie dropped back to side Morgan. The older man looked to be almost asleep in the saddle. Morgan slowed Brag, and Willie's mount followed suit. "Hey," Morgan called. "Don't fall."

Willie opened an eye and snorted. "Ain't likely, son."

"Those rocks tonight were the strangest formation I've ever seen." Morgan kept his voice loud enough only for the other cowboy to make out. "It's possible any or all of the outlaws could have hidden, but to escape completely? Don't see how."

Yet the men had returned from climbing the rock clusters to report that no one was there. He'd started to search the formations himself before Ray called everyone together to herd the cattle home.

"Another damned, ball-bustin' ride is what it was. And all for nothin'. I'm gonna sleep till noon, and if the boss comes out before then, he can wait." Will snorted.

"Is it always like this, or was today different?" Morgan asked.

"Hell, we ain't never caught even a solitary one of the devils doin' this," Willie said. "We're good at findin' the stock, usually, but never a body do we drag back to the sheriff. Boss don't like the idea of killin' anybody, even a dirty thief."

"But this time a rancher died, didn't he? Has that happened before?"

"Nah. Old Sven's the first. Mostly they grab whatever animals they can find and be off."

"That must be why the boss said to bring them back in any shape."

"Likely so. He was right mad we didn't get old Bobby. Reckon he'll have somethin' to say about that when he comes out."

They rode in silence for a bit before Morgan asked, "How many jobs have they pulled around here?"

Willie thought for a minute. "Happened once or twice afore this year. But since Christmas time, they's been…let's see…six, I reckon. Then there's the Olsens, that's seven. Tall T, Triangle A, Rocking C—those had the stock found and brought back."

"And you've always found the stock but not the rustlers?"

"Not always. The Gordons and old man Simpson and the Pierce family—their animals got clean away. Another 'un south of here. Sheriff got some of them cattle back, but the family sold up anyhow. Left last spring."

"Right odd, the cattle found for the big ranchers but not the little ones."

"Son, I learned long time ago not to notice *odd*. You'll be happier that way."

"So, what do you figure? A crew of four, maybe five? Bigger crew could handle more animals."

Willie grunted. Another silence stretched until Morgan said, "Rustling's a problem lots of places. I saw a good deal of it in Texas. Took months to find one gang. Good thing the sheriff was along when we did. I don't think the rest of the boys would have bothered hauling them back to jail."

"Yeah, old Sheriff Hanson wouldn't take kindly to vigilante justice. He's a stickler. And as I said, the boss don't hold with no killin' neither."

"Good to know," Morgan said. And interesting. Seeing what Foster specifically told Morgan about Bobby Bullseye.

Too many pieces turned sideways in this puzzle.

Chapter 14

Deciding to go as she was, work dress and all, Emily closed the office and stopped by the hotel for supper. She sat at a small table near the back, well away from the window and door. Only one other table was occupied, also toward the back.

She smiled when the waitress came to take her order. "It's been a long day. Do you know what sounds good? Eggs and bacon. Would that be possible? And are there any of those wonderful biscuits left from this morning?"

"Sounds simple enough, Miss Martin. And yes to the biscuits. Cook makes 'em all day. They're right popular." The waitress poured a cup of coffee and turned away.

"Good evening."

Emily glanced up to find the talkative man from the train, Eli Foster. He gestured to the table. "May I join you? I hate to see a lovely lady dine alone."

She nodded and indicated the place opposite. He removed his hat and put it in an empty chair. Before he sat, he lifted a hand to summon the waitress.

As if she can't see for herself someone else is here.

He settled into his seat and smiled. "I believe we met briefly a few days ago, but let me introduce myself again. I'm Eli Foster."

Emily used her pleasant-but-distant social smile. "I

do remember you, Mr. Foster. I'm Miss Emily Martin. My brother, David, runs *The Wylder Sun*."

"Pleased to meet you, Miss Martin. I was sorry to hear that your brother left town before you arrived. I'm sure being in a new and unfamiliar place must be difficult. Will you be going home soon?"

"Thank you for your concern, but I agreed to wait for David. I'm looking forward to joining him with the newspaper."

She longed to ask about the search last night. Why he sent his men along with the sheriff. But that might betray her source. She felt oddly protective of Morgan Dodd.

Instead, she said, "I believe you told me you are an agent for the Union Pacific? That must keep you quite busy. On my trip here, I found the railway to be quite responsive to its customers' needs."

"We do our best to provide every comfort to our travelers. After all, without folks like you, we wouldn't be in business." He chuckled on the heels of his condescending comment.

"And business must be quite good. I understand the company is expanding rapidly?"

"Ah, yes." His startled expression shouldn't have surprised her. He likely was another of those men who thought women's main functions were to grace their arms, birth their children, and run their homes.

"The new rolling mill in Laramie has been successful in recycling the company's soft iron rails that are being replaced, I understand."

He stared at her, his mouth ajar. Before he could reply, the waitress arrived to pour his coffee. He gave his order, and when the girl had scurried away, he focused his attention on Emily.

He really wasn't a bad looking fellow at all. Strands of gray at his temples lent him a rather distinguished air.

"Let me say, I am impressed," he said. "I've never before met a young lady with such knowledge of the rail industry. Is your father a railroad man?"

"Oh, no. Father is an attorney, but our newspapers in Kansas City provide a thorough coverage of issues from throughout the country. And territories."

"Of course. Your brother was known for his interest in business in these parts. It must run in the family."

Emily smiled, a genuine one this time. "I do enjoy writing about topics of importance."

"That's delightful. The women of Wylder will be happy to have their hobbies covered in the local paper. I heard that the *Sun* had some bad luck after your brother left. Will he back soon? Is the press still operational?"

"There was some vandalism, but I've begun cleaning up with the help of an industrious young man in town."

"You must mean Tommy. I saw him and his friend in here gathering biscuits and coffee this morning."

They were interrupted when the waitress arrived with their meals. After she left again, Foster leaned forward. "Miss Martin, I would be happy to help with any cleaning or repairs you have. Just say the word, and I'll send some men over tomorrow."

"I believe everything is taken care of. But it's a kind offer," Emily said. And it was. She wondered if she'd misjudged him.

"Happy to help. Just let me know. My position

with the railroad has a great deal to do with land. Because of that, I have to be away from town for a day or so. When I get back, I will be available to lend a hand myself."

Emily smiled her thanks. From there the conversation moved to what the town had to offer in shops and entertainment, and she finished the meal pleasantly. When a man introduced as a member of the town council stopped to talk with Foster, she said, "I hope you will excuse me, gentlemen, but the day has been exhausting. There are a few things I must finish tonight."

She discreetly placed her payment next to her plate and rose before Foster could notice and insist upon paying for her meal. "It's been a pleasure to meet you both. I bid you goodnight."

As she walked away, a weight lifted from her chest. This evening had brought several things to consider, not the least of which was the contradiction that Eli Foster presented. But for now, she wanted simply to rest. A bath would be heaven, but collecting and heating enough water was beyond her energies. Tomorrow night, she vowed, she'd treat herself to a long soak.

Light from the setting sun still limned the western horizon when she gingerly stretched out on the bed, kitty tucked on the opposed side of the pillow. She fell asleep instantly.

Emily arrived at the office before eight the next morning, carrying bucket, mop, and broom. She wore her oldest bodice and skirt, which was to say, last season's. Surveying her clothing earlier, she'd realized that nothing she'd brought would be appropriate for physical labor. There was a dressmaker somewhere near—she recalled seeing the sign. Perhaps she could get some work gowns made.

She tied a cloth around her waist and set to with the broom. It wasn't long before it became obvious she should have worn gloves. By the time she'd reached the back of the office and swept the last bit of dirt onto a paper to dump into the refuse keg, her palms were red and stinging.

Nearly ten o'clock. She'd swept and dusted for nearly two hours. Time for a break. She removed the apron, washed her hands, and set out for the bakery.

Cissy met her with a wide smile and a bright, "'Morning. I've got coffee on. How about some?"

Emily actually groaned. "Perfect. I need reviving."

"Sit yourself down. I'll bring it right out."

It wasn't long before Cissy joined her at the table with a tray loaded with two mugs, sugar, milk, spoons, and two slices of apple pie.

While the coffee cooled to sipping temperature, Emily filled her in on the past two days, minus mention of her handsome escort on the journey back from Cheyenne. When she reached for her cup, Cissy grabbed her hand.

"My goodness. You need gloves or your hands will be bleeding before you're done."

"I realized that too late. I'll go to the house and get some before I start scrubbing."

Cissy's eyes narrowed in question. "Have you ever used a scrub mob before?"

"Of course. That is, it can't be much different from using a broom, can it?"

"Oh, my. Look, I know some girls who would be

happy to help out for a little pay. Why don't you let me send word to one of them?"

"That's very kind, but this is something I need to do myself," Emily insisted.

Cissy sat back. "If you intend to prove something to yourself, I won't interfere. But I have a spare pair of cotton gloves I use for the oven. You take those for the afternoon."

When Emily started to protest, Cissy said, "Now don't be arguing. Friends help each other out, don't they? Besides—"

Her words stopped as she looked past Emily's shoulder and out onto the street. Emily turned to see a large wagon piled with assorted furniture and trunks. On the front seat sat a middle-aged man and woman. Behind them, on the second hard board bench, were a boy and girl. Both appeared to be nearing their teen years. The wagon pulled in by the bank.

Emily swung around to peer at Cissy. "What's wrong?"

"Those are the Gordons. Are they moving out? I'll be right back." She jumped up and dashed out the door.

Emily rose and followed, although slower. Gordon. Wasn't that the name of the family the boys sent biscuits to yesterday? And the one Morgan visited the day he drove her back from Cheyenne? Perhaps with the loss of all their stock, they'd decided to give up.

As she reached the other side of the street, the man entered the bank. Cissy stood beside the woman, speaking in low tones. The woman didn't reply, simply stared ahead.

"Ma ain't herself today," the girl said, her voice anxious. "Packin's been right tirin' for her."

Cissy stepped along the side of the wagon to better talk to the girl. "Where you moving?"

"We're goin' back to Illinois," the girl answered. "Right now, we're for Cheyenne. We plan to sell the furniture there, then take the train."

"I'm so sorry to hear you are leaving," Emily said. "I'm Miss Martin. I'm new to town, but I heard that rustlers took your cattle last week."

The boy snorted and folded his arms. "Damn thieves," he said. "Don't know why Sheriff Hanson can't put a stop to 'em. We shouldn't have to leave. It's our property, our right to stay. Ma and Pa bought the land from the railroad. It's ours."

"Jamie," his sister cautioned. "You know what Pa said."

The boy threw her a disgusted frown and ducked his head.

Emily glanced at Cissy, whose face creased in concern. The bank door creaked open, and Gordon stepped out, his gait slow, his weathered face solemn.

"Miz Standish." His nod took in both Cissy and Emily.

"Mr. Gordon, I'm sorry to see you are leaving us," Cissy said. "Is there anything we can do for you?"

"I thank you, but we had enough." He stopped along the other side of the wagon, his voice lowered. "Ma, here, ain't doing too well. I'm takin' her back to her family in Illinois. 'Spect that'll cheer her up. Thanks to Mr. Foster, we got enough for a start back there."

"*No* thanks to Mr. Foster, don't you mean, Pa? He didn't offer near enough for our place. Even I know that. He ain't no angel of mercy like you been carryin' on. He's the devil, that's what."

"Quiet, boy!" Gordon's command carried weight if not volume. "We're not arguin' about this no more. Your ma's sick, and she needs the kind of attention we can't get out here. Doc said himself she might perk up if she was back among her kinfolk. That's what we're doing."

Jamie leaped from the wagon and stalked a few feet into the street, forcing a rider to detour around him.

"Tell you what," Cissy said, "if I can't do anything else, I can send some nice bread with you. Just wait right here, Mr. Gordon. I know your missus likes my cherry pie, and I have one cooling right now. Jamie, you come along with me while I make up a basket for your ride to Cheyenne."

When Gordon made to object, Cissy said, "Now, no argument. Won't be long. Come on, Jamie."

Emily fell in beside the two as they hurried back to the bakery.

"How long has your mother been ill, Jamie?" Emily asked.

"Since the day the news came that we weren't gettin' our stock back." Jamie eyed her. "You're Tommy's friend, the one he was workin' for at the newspaper."

"That's right. He'll be sorry to see you go, I know."

"It ain't right. Mr. Foster bought Pa out for nothin'," Jamie muttered, loud enough for the two women to hear. "He cheated us, and Pa thinks we ought to be grateful."

"But if he's made it possible for your family to start over in a place your mother is familiar with, isn't that a good thing?"

He didn't say a word until they were inside the bakery and the door shut. Then, "Not near enough. It's not like Pa homesteaded. He paid for the land, and look what's there now. A house, two trees for shade, a corral, a chicken house, a tool shed, a garden planted. A barn, 'till it burned. And lots of land. Good land. Land's expensive back East, and cattle and horses and plows. Pa's goin' to have to go into debt for a lot of it. And he shouldn't have to."

"Still, it seems nice of Mr. Foster to buy a house and land when he already has a large ranch, I understand."

"Yeah. Well. He owns the parcel one over from us, too, on the other side of the railroad's. Jim Stone used to live there, but he got raided last winter. Weren't nobody but Mr. Stone lived there. He were plannin' to go back to Chicago and marry his lady, but he told Pa she wouldn't come out to such a wild place now, so he's workin' in her family's store in the city. Mr. Foster bought him out too."

Cissy came from the back, carrying two loaves of still-warm bread and a pie, all wrapped in newspaper and resting in a basket. "I cut the pie in slices, but you might want to be careful. Wait to eat it till the filling sets up and it isn't so messy."

Eyes wide, the boy took the food. "Thank you," he said. "You always been nice to us."

His eyes suspiciously glassy, he turned, and Emily opened the door for him.

"And Jamie, there's a few molasses cookies in there for you and your sister. Be careful, lad."

The two women watched him make his way back

to the wagon and hand the food up to his sister. Mr. Gordon glanced over his shoulder at the shop, raised the whip in thanks, and the wagon lurched forward. The bakery was silent for a few minutes, then the two moved back to their table. The coffee was cool by that time, but Emily didn't mind.

Cissy's kindness touched her greatly. "You're very generous."

"I hate to see a family that's been here a while have to give up. It's like they were run out because of bad luck. They're the second family, besides Stone, that's headed back since spring."

Emily hadn't thought about the dangers of life here. She hadn't considered that Wylder was on a kind of frontier. David always talked about the affluence of Cheyenne and all the development around it. She'd assumed that stability had extended to Wylder. She hadn't considered what the land beyond the city was like.

"You look troubled," Cissy said. "Didn't expect the roughness? I didn't either. I grew up in Chicago, until my situation became impossible. When I came out here, I was surprised."

"But you've adapted so well," Emily said.

"So will you." Cissy smiled. "Eat up. Then I'll show you where to get some reasonable clothes made."

Emily laughed. "You read my mind. I suppose I didn't have a clear idea of what life would be like here. David's descriptions were rather misleading."

"Men." Cissy shook her head, laughing. "You'll have to come back tomorrow and tell me what you think of our dressmaker, Widow Lowery."

She handed Emily the cotton gloves and explained

how to find the dressmaker's shop. Emily left feeling better, calmer than she had when she arrived. Having a friend made all the difference.

Her mind conjured up the image of Morgan Dodd, the memory of that brief kiss, of his warm body pressed against hers. Of the scent of horse and leather and musk. She couldn't consider him a friend. Her stomach took a little dip and despite the sun, a shiver skittered across her shoulders.

Could she?

Chapter 15

The next morning, Emily stood before the Widow Lowery, waiting to have the last of her measurements taken for three new dresses. Work dresses, the shop owner called them. What all females out West ought to wear, if they had any sense, she said.

"Simple, that's what you want," she declared. A no-nonsense woman, Emily had discovered immediately. The seamstress pushed up Emily's elbow "Hold up that arm."

Emily winced.

"I'll swan to goodness, you're the flinchingest female I ever saw." Mrs. Lowery slapped the tape measure against Emily's side. "If you're that touchy, maybe you ought go on back East. This ain't no place for a woman who can't even stand up for a dress fitting."

Emily didn't know what to say. She'd never before been scolded by the proprietor of a business wanting her custom.

Should she be offended, or take the words in stride? She opted for a straight answer.

"To tell the truth, I think every muscle in my body is rebelling today," she said. "I scrubbed floors yesterday until my fingers were numb. I admit, it's been a good while since I moved heavy furniture."

"Huh. Little hard work never hurt a body. Out of

practice, are you?" Mrs. Lowery nudged Emily's side. "Turn the other way. That's right."

She measured from Emily's waist to her ankles, then wound the tape measure around her own wrist and jotted down some numbers in a small notebook lying on a table.

She tossed down the pencil. "Let me see. Come on. What have you done to yourself?"

Emily gingerly extended her hands. Blisters bubbled along the sides and at the base of both thumbs and dotted her right palm. Mrs. Lowery let out a disgusted huff. "Go on downstairs to the laundry room. Leona can fix you up with some ointment she used to use. And girl, if you're going stay in Wylder, get somebody who knows what they're doing to help you out."

By now, Emily had learned, nearly everyone along the main street knew who she was and why she was in town. If Mrs. Lowery's attitude was any indication, most of them thought she didn't belong here.

She didn't give a darn. Here she was, and no matter how long it took for David to return, here she would stay.

A moan slipped from between her clenched lips as she maneuvered her skirt on over her petticoat. Dreading the thought of wrestling into her bodice, she reached for it draped on the back of a chair, but slightly rough fingers pushed her hand away.

"Let me," Widow Lowery grumbled, "or you won't be dressed in time for supper."

When she'd arrived shortly after eight a.m. Emily had been taken aback by the strident attitude that greeted her. Rude, she'd labeled the widow. But she had no choice. She didn't have time to sew her own dresses, what with getting the supplies ready for the office.

It hadn't taken Emily long to peg the woman, though. Irascible but very good at what she did. And, Emily suspected, possessing a very well-hidden soft spot.

The woman helped her on with the bodice and buttoned the front for her. "Don't know what you were thinking, bringing none but fancy day gowns with you. You can't ride a horse in that outfit. And if you plan to mess around with that press at all, you'll ruin every one of those ruffly skirts. Now," she said, turning away, "I'll have one of those dresses ready in a couple of days or so. Maybe three. I got another order to finish first."

She picked up a gown lying on an overstuffed chair. The shiny green fabric rustled as she settled it across her knees to hem.

"That's beautiful material," Emily said.

"Thanks, honey."

Startled, Emily turned to the doorway to find a lovely redhead stepping into the shop.

"You must be David's little sister," the woman said, walking farther inside. "I'm Ruby. He said you was comin' to visit. When's he gettin' back, do you know? We sure are missin' his handsome face down at the Social Club."

"Miss Ruby." Emily inclined her head. "I'm glad to meet another friend of David's. I don't know when he'll return."

Ruby stepped across to a chair and sat. "You found that good-for-nothin' Charlie yet? I hear tell he took off for Cheyenne. Bet he'll come back to work if you ask him. Doin' for a daily newspaper is likely more work than he's used to."

Before Emily could answer, Mrs. Lowery stood. "Try this on now, Ruby. I think the length is right."

Without another word, the other woman slid out of the cotton dress she wore. Emily nearly choked when she glimpsed the fancy underpinnings. Embroidered pink corset, laced tightly over a sleeveless ruffled chemisette; silk pantalettes ending at mid-calf and trimmed in lace, also all pink. It ought to have clashed with the red hair, but oddly, it didn't. And no petticoats.

The green dress shimmered over her head and down her body. It fit very well. Perhaps a bit tight through the hips, however. And short. Her ankles were visible.

Ruby peered at herself in the long mirror propped against one wall. She turned, walked away while glancing over her shoulder at the reflection of her swaying hips beneath the rustling fabric, then turned again and walked back, all the while examining the effect of the gown.

She smiled. "Perfect. Except..." She frowned into the mirror and tugged at the neckline, already sitting low on her breasts. "A little high, ain't it? You know how I like them."

Mrs. Lowery unfastened the back of the gown, and the woman stepped out of it. As she put on her other dress, she glanced at Emily. "I hear the Gordons left. You see them go?"

"Yesterday," Emily said. "They were on the way to Illinois, I believe."

"Damn shame if you ask me," she said. "The girls were talkin' this mornin' that Eli Foster bought them out." The edge to her voice told Emily more than her words did.

"Is that bad?" she asked.

"Oh, honey, I don't know a thing about the price of farms or ranches or cattle. Just seems like he's accumulated an awful lot of all three, here in the last year or so."

Mrs. Lowery cleared her throat. "Now Ruby, you don't want to be talking out of turn. Word is, Eli Foster's gonna run for mayor."

Ruby's eyebrows shot up, and her mouth fell open. "Never say so." Her laughter was genuine, loud, and ended quick. "Don't mayors have to live in town? No matter how fast Wylder's growin', it ain't takin' in that ranch of his five miles away."

"Well, now, could be he's giving his town residence as the Social Club," Mrs. Lowery said. With pursed mouth, she could have been making an insult, but Emily had the distinct impression the quip was meant as a joke. Ruby took it that way too.

"Damn if he don't spend enough time there to qualify," she said, laughing again. "But I'm sure as hell not claimin' him."

Election for mayor? Emily wondered at that. "When are city elections held here?"

"Huh. When was the last time we had an election?" Mrs. Lowery asked.

Ruby thought for a moment. "Can't recall. Wait. Grady was the last mayor, but he moved to Cheyenne. Haven't had one since. What's that, then…three years, four? Town council usually decides things, them and the sheriff and the pastor."

"Why is he running then?" Emily asked.

The two other women exchanged glances. Ruby raised her expressive eyebrows. "Got me. But that's a mighty good question. Too bad David ain't back yet. He'd get to the bottom of it." She moved to the door, then glanced at Emily again. "Welcome to Wylder, Miss Martin."

"I'm Emily."

Ruby smiled her genuine smile. "Glad to hear it, Emily. You take care, now." She looked over at the seamstress. "Want me to close the door or leave it open?"

"Close it. Enough flies come in through the windows."

Silence fell in her wake. After a moment, Emily said, "She mentioned the Social Club?"

"The Wylder County Social Club is a gathering place for men." Mrs. Lowrey's voice carried an odd lilt.

Emily thought of the clubs her father and Randolph belonged to. But somehow she didn't think that was the kind of...

"Oh." Her face burned.

"Yep."

Before Mrs. Lowery could explain further, the door swung open again. The woman who stepped in wore a one-piece blue checked gown that buttoned halfway down the front. That must be the kind of sensible dress Emily would be wearing soon.

"Goodness me, Mildred Lowery," the newcomer huffed. "Did I just pass one of Those Women coming from here?"

"Maddie, I sew for whoever needs clothes," Mrs. Lowery said. "You know that. And don't be acting like she has typhus. She dresses respectable when she's in town, don't she?"

"It don't matter what she wears in the daytime, it's what she and her kind wear at night that's so scandalous. And to think she goes about just like the rest of us."

"Now, Maddie, let's not fuss about who my customers are. If you don't like them, you know you can go somewheres else."

"And you know nobody else can cut a dress like you," Maddie grumbled. "The least you could do is set special hours for those girls if you have to do for them."

"Come on, now, it's too hot to fret," the widow said. She glanced at Emily. "Don't forget that ointment. Come back in a couple days, all right?"

Emily nodded and slipped out of the shop, grateful when a breeze found her on the outside stairway. "Ow," she whispered when she stepped off the first step. Her legs were sore and cramping from yesterday's strains too. *Why in all that's holy did I think I could take my first try at cleaning all in one day? 'How hard can it be?' Famous last words.*

By the time the last stair step had been conquered, Emily was biting her lips at the growing pain. She might as well go home and rest. Organizing the office had to wait until tomorrow. Surely she'd feel better then.

A half hour later, carrying a stoppered bottle of ointment and a sandwich from the hotel restaurant, Emily straggled into the house. She locked the door, removed her skirt, petticoat, bodice, stockings, and shoes. Kitty made a game of it, weaving between Emily's feet. But when Emily tried to stoop down and pet the mite, pain jabbed her lower back.

After slathering ointment on her hands, shoulders, and legs, she stretched out on the bed. And gasped.

Which would be worse—to suffer the aches and pains or smell the noxious substance covering her? Even kitty kept to her towel bed on the floor.

But before long, the odor began to dissipate, and warmth tingled along Emily's skin.

Finally, she slept.

Chapter 16

He was a damn fool.

Morgan stood in the doorway of *The Wylder Sun*, staring at the back of the lady seated at the desk. A lady as far removed from him as his childhood innocence. He still had time to turn, take Brag, ride out like he should have done hours ago.

But no. He'd had to take the long way north and ride into town, like he was attached to an invisible cord, just to see if she was in the office. For what? To say goodbye? Why the hell would she care if he left? God only knew when he'd be back. Or if.

He shifted, both uneasy and guilty at that last thought. Sounded too much like he doubted himself. No if's when he went on a job. No maybes. He did it. He always did it.

He lifted his hand to knock on the door frame. Paused again. Damn. He had to admit it. Something inside him had changed over the past months. Couldn't put his finger on exactly when, he just knew. Knew this would be his last job. Knew he wanted to come home to something, to someone.

And deep inside, he knew such thinking got a man killed.

Hell. He didn't want to think about it anymore.

He knocked.

"Is this a bad time?" His voice surprised even

himself in the silence.

She jerked and glanced over a shoulder. "Not at all."

"You looked pained when you turned your head."

"That's because I turned my head." A groan mixed with her short laugh. "Come in, please. I'm still suffering the effects from a day of cleaning and mopping. Goodness, I hate to admit such a normal thing makes me ache so. Yesterday I could hardly move, but thanks to a miracle cream from Leona at Mrs. Lowery's, it's much better today."

Morgan dragged one of the two remaining chairs to the end of the desk and sat facing the opposite direction where he could see her face. If he judged right, Miss Emily Martin had never scrubbed a floor before in her sheltered life. He recalled his mother's Saturday ritual of cleaning and knew it wasn't an easy chore. No wonder Miss Martin felt the aftereffects.

"What brings you to town this morning?" she asked, rescuing him from his memories. Seemed like he'd been cursed with thoughts of the old days way too much lately. If he didn't focus, this damn well *would* be his last job.

"I'm heading north for Eli Foster." He tossed his hat on the desk and leaned back. "Don't know how long I'll be gone, and I wanted to pick up a few things at the Mercantile before I left. When I noticed your door open, I thought I'd check on how your cleaning's coming."

Noticed the door open, his foot. He'd ridden out of the way to find her there. He didn't need to stop in town. But for some reason he refused to explore too deeply, he'd wanted to see her before he left.

"All finished." She straightened her shoulders. "Now I'm ready to put out a paper. Well, almost."

With a fingertip, she nudged her sheet of paper his way. That's when he noticed she wore a white cotton glove on one hand. Odd.

"Here's a list of what remains to be done. It's"—her voice roughened, and she coughed—"short. The press frames have been repaired and the metal straightened. All I need is a typesetter. And some ads. And some ink. And some paper."

She gave a short, discouraged laugh.

He didn't like seeing her so downcast. He placed a hand on her shoulder. "It'll come together. Don't fret. Look at me."

She swung her upper body toward him—and uttered a laughing, "Ooouch." She lifted her ungloved hand to rub her shoulder, and Morgan froze. He grabbed her fingers.

"What in hell have you done to yourself?" She winced at his rough voice. He smoothed his thumb across her blistered palm, then took her other hand and removed the glove. A thin bandage wound around her palm and thumb.

"Cissy loaned me some gloves, but wringing out a mop was awkward. So..."

"You didn't use them." He shook his head, stood, and pulled her up. "Come here."

Standing behind her, he kneaded her shoulders and back. She angled her head and gave a long sigh. He took a half-step closer, near enough to feel the heat of her body, smell the fragrance of her soap—and the rank tang of the ointment. He inched his head closer to her hair. No ointment there, just a soft scent of flowers, of…sweetness. He inhaled deeply. He longed to pull her against him, slide his arms around her waist, brush his lips along the side of her throat.

Her muscles stiffened, and she stepped away from his touch. Had she sensed the way she stirred him? Maybe she didn't like the feel of his rough hands. And why would she? He was a gun for hire; she was a lady.

But when she turned to pick up the sheet of notes, her cheeks were flushed, and her chest rose and fell quickly.

Could it be she felt the same pull as he did? She cleared her throat.

"Thank you. I feel much better now." She shot him a quick side glance. "I don't suppose you know how to put a press together?"

I need to be on the trail. "Never tried before, but let's see what's back there."

The process turned out to be not as bad as he'd feared. Easy to spot where the pieces went, but attaching them was tricky. Every part had to be set solidly in place or the contraption wouldn't run, she insisted. Well, she should know.

The last section, the flat container for the paper, attached beneath the press. He lay on his back, as far beneath the metal base as his chest allowed.

"Hand me that big metal clamp, would you?"

"This one?" she asked.

He angled to the right but couldn't see which she held. He lifted his head for a better look—right into the metal undercarriage of the machine. "Damn."

A muffled sound reached him as he lay back. "Are you laughing?"

"Oh no," came a strangled voice, followed by a

giggle. "Sorry. Here, I'll bring it to you."

Before he could warn her to stay put, she wriggled on her stomach to his side, whispering "Ow, ow, ow." Holding the clamp in his line of vision, she asked, "Is this the right one?"

"Turn it. I can't see through the bandage. That's it. Slide it between my thumb and forefinger. I've got to hold this plate firm, or it won't attach flat enough."

A warm weight slid across his chest. What the hell…she was laying her head on his chest?

"I see where it goes," she said. "You keep the plate in place, and I'll set the clamp."

"Don't try that. I know you're hurting."

"No, no. I'm fine."

She was lying through her gritted teeth, but what could he do? Stubborn woman. In between bursts of the noxious ointment, he caught the light fragrance of flowers.

Which would have been bad enough if she hadn't then twisted onto her back—stifling a moan, he swore—to tuck a hand between each at his on the connection he held. With a few more wriggles, she had the clamp loosely in place.

"There," she said. "I'll move now, and you can tighten it." What followed was the worst minute Morgan had suffered in recent years. Still moving awkwardly and wincing from occasional pain, the woman inched herself back down his chest and stomach until her head bumped his belt buckle. Then she eased from beneath his still-bent arm and out from under the press.

God in heaven. If she'd turned her head to the side, she would've had the surprise of her life. And he'd

127

likely embarrass himself in a way he hadn't since he was thirteen. His swollen cock ached like a—well, there was nothing that hurt with the pleasureful pain of an unresolved hard-on.

"Can you get it fastened?" she said, stooping to peer at him

He grunted and tightened the clamp. "Stand back, I'm coming out."

When he managed to roll from under the press and rise, she stood on the other side, testing a lever. After a moment, she gave a brilliant smile and practically ran to him. "You did it. It's ready to go. Thank you so much, Mr. Dodd."

****

Emily hadn't meant to collide with him, but her unexpected movement had brought on another series of pains. He stepped forward at the wrong time, and she came flat up against him. His arms snapped around her waist, he took a faltering few steps backward and slammed against the heavy bookcase separating the two ends of the room. When they stopped moving, her hands clutched against his chest, and her body pressed to his.

She took a breath to apologize, but when she looked into his eyes, no words came. His gaze slid to her mouth. And she knew he was going to kiss her. Her breath hitched.

Pull away, Emily. You do not want this.
Yes. I do.

While she debated with herself, his lips brushed hers, and all thought left her. Only sensations remained. His lips moving over hers. Gentle. Soft. The whiff of shaving soap. Spicy. Not sweet like Randolph's. The warmth of his breath against her skin as he lifted his head just enough to look into her eyes. She answered by rising on her toes, fitting her mouth to his. This time, his kiss was firm, deep, searching. Her heart pounded in her ears and in time with his, thudding against her fingers.

He pulled her closer. She slid her arms around his waist, hands moving up his back, fingers circling in the ways his had earlier when he'd soothed her aching muscles. She forgot all about her discomfort in the overwhelming rush of sensations.

Giving a muffled curse, he jerked his head up, pressing his chin against her hair, rocking her back and forth. His breath came in gulps. His body was like a steel wall, his muscles tense, tight. Against her stomach, she felt the throb of his cock through all their clothing.

Her own breath came ragged and shallow. She trembled from the unexpected vehemence of her reaction. Never had she experienced anything like the avalanche of confused emotions, not from a simple kiss and embrace. Nothing in her months-long engagement to Randolph had prepared her for such overpowering feelings.

He held her while they regained a semblance of control, until she stepped back.

"I...I...don't know what to say," she murmured.

"Neither do I."

The surprise that rang in his low voice brought her gaze back to his face. He looked exposed. Stunned.

"Hey! Anybody there?"

The shout triggered a yelp from Emily, and she tripped as she took a quick step back.

"Be right there," she called, still looking at Morgan. He reached out and straightened her bodice, then winked.

Heavy steps thudded on the wooden floor up front. She inhaled a long, steady breath and rounded the bookcase. "May I help you?"

Chapter 17

"Miss Martin, ma'am?"

Emily stepped around the bookcase and stopped. "Charlie? Oh, my. I'm so happy you're here." Still emotional from Morgan's embrace, she feared she'd tear up at the unexpected appearance. Then a fear struck her. "You have come back to stay, haven't you?"

"Yes, ma'am. If'n you still need me." He snatched off his cap.

"Of course I do. There will be no *Sun* without you."

A tinge of pink colored his weathered face, and they both laughed.

"That sounded odd, didn't it," she said. "You know what I meant."

"Yes 'um. Uh. Wasn't sure what we needed, but I recollected what the place looked like last time I was in. Figured we'd need some supplies. So's I brought a barrel of ink and some paper, out in the wagon."

"That's wonderful. Exactly the right things. Mr. Dodd just finished putting the press together."

Morgan walked past them and plucked his hat from the desk. "If that's all, Miss Martin, I'll be on my way."

Emily's stomach leapt. Surely he wasn't leaving like this. "My thanks for your help, sir. Wait one moment for your payment."

Ignoring his mutters, she reached for her reticule in

the bottom desk drawer. Fiddling with the drawstrings, she moved toward the open door. Morgan gained her side and put a hand over the drawstrings. "No pay needed, ma'am. My pleasure to help out. I'm riding on now."

His voice had been pitched loudly enough to reach Charlie, but then he lowered it for her ears only. "I'll see you when I get back." Hand still on her bag, he stroked a finger across her knuckles.

His gritty whisper raked her spine, and she shivered. Her voice caught. "Yes, please. You'll be careful?"

Her gaze searched his face, then caught on the searing intensity of his eyes. His mouth leveled into grim line. "I will."

Giving a nod, he ambled to the tie rail where his horse waited. At right angles to the mount sat a loaded buckboard. The side carried a painted name, "Strong's Livery, Cheyenne."

Morgan swung into the saddle, touched the brim of his hat to her, and rode away.

Emily stroked her knuckles where his caress had landed. Oh goodness, she couldn't stand here, watching him ride away. What if someone saw her, mooning like a…well. She wasn't daft, merely surprised.

"Ma'am?" Charlie had come to stand beside her. "That there's the wagon I brought over with supplies."

"I was looking at that, Charlie, and thinking where it all should go."

"Oh, I'll take care of that, ma'am. I know where to stash it."

Emily looked at the typesetter to whom David attributed so much of the paper's success. "Each time you say ma'am, I expect to see my mother nearby. Perhaps you might call me Emily?"

"Oh, no, ma'am, that wouldn't be respectful." He frowned, thought a moment, then said, "I could call you Miss Emily."

She smiled. "Fine, Charlie. Now, while you and the driver unload, I'll start gathering ads and news." She started back into the office for her small notebook, then thought of something else. "Do you have a place to live?"

"I stay over to the Boardin' House."

"Culpepper's?"

"That's right. Serves a right good breakfast, she does, if'n you're not late. So I always get to work early."

"Wonderful. We'll settle more details later. For now, let me say again how very pleased I am to see you." Smiling at the man, whose wrinkled face again flushed pink, she went inside. It would be wise to read several back issues of the paper to see what David had covered in the past, and she'd intended to do just that. Except she somehow hadn't gotten to it. Later today. She might even take a few home with her tonight. Satisfied, she grabbed the notebook and set out.

She began her rounds with someone familiar. Cissy, who gladly bought a small ad. The two chatted briefly about goings-on in the town, until more customers bombarded the shop.

Next stop, the hotel. "Don't need to advertise. Everybody around here knows where we are," was her answer from Mr. Diamond, the current manager. "And I don't rightly see how the restaurant could handle more customers."

"Don't you have a meeting room?" she asked. "Perhaps groups would like to make use of that."

"What groups? Oh, you mean like the town council? They already do, sometimes. Once a month or so, they have dinner here and talk over what's to be done."

That reminded her. "I understand there's to be a special election for mayor. Do you know who is running? Has the council talked about it here?"

"Well, now, you better ask someone else about that. I couldn't say."

"I heard Mr. Foster is a candidate. He lives here in the hotel, doesn't he? When he's not at his ranch?"

"Ma'am, I don't talk about our guests. But just so you know, he's here temporary-like, while he builds a place in town. Permanent. Like he says, his business with the railroad makes him a city man. It's in his and the Union Pacific's interest to see Wylder grow like it ought to."

Emily moved closer to the registration counter and lowered her voice. "That's so right," she said. "I've been here just a few days, but already I see how important the railroad is. Why I heard that Wylder is closer to the cattle trail than Cheyenne. Perhaps…"

The clerk gave a smug smile at those words. He looked fit to burst with all the information swelling his chest.

She nodded. "It sounds like he's a forward-thinking man. Well, then, I should go. But I do hope you will mention to the owner that even a few words in the paper would remind people of how essential the hotel is to Wylder's future."

By the time she'd closed her notebook, the clerk's

sullen attitude had eased. "I'll mention it to him, Miss Martin."

Outside, she considered her next stop. The hotel's refusal disappointed her, but perhaps in the future, the owner would relent. Mrs. Lowery's was close. She might as well try there. Apparently, Mrs. Lowery was in the seamstresses' room again, and as Emily climbed the stairway, she heard raised voices.

Hand on the latch, she paused. "You ought to go see Doc Sullivan," came Mrs. Lowery's strident tones. Emily pushed open the door just a crack

Ruby, the lady she'd met there earlier from the Social Club, modeled the green dress, complete with a dramatically lowered neckline. But Emily's gaze was caught not on the décolletage, but the bruises rising above it. Gasping, she saw the downturned face.

The woman's bottom lip was swollen and split on one side. This, apparently, is what the doctor needed to attend to. Emily judged the wound could use a stitch or two.

"Don't make no fuss over this," Ruby said. "You know he ain't done anythin' like it for a long time. And it wouldn't have happened last night if I hadn't smarted off at him about the election. I know what he's like when he's had too much of his fancy whiskey."

"Why the dickens would he be mad about the election? He's always had it in his pocket," Mrs. Lowery muttered.

"You didn't hear? Mr. Holden's signed up to run against him."

"Not Horace Holden? Lordy, what's that man thinking? He's got no right, looking to lead a town like this."

Emily couldn't stand there eavesdropping indefinitely. Besides, she wanted details of what the women were talking about. Giving a quick knock, she pushed open the door.

"Good morning. I hope I'm not interrupting." A surreptitious glance at Ruby confirmed what she'd glimpsed earlier. The woman's cheek was puffy and the lower part of her jaw next to her split lip was a dark blue tinged with purple.

The conversation stopped when she entered. Then Mrs. Lowery said, "Don't have your dress done yet."

"I didn't come for that. We're getting ready to print a paper, and I'm gathering ads and information."

"That good-for-nothing Charlie finally show up, did he? 'Bout time if you ask me. I don't advertise. Got enough business as is. Couldn't handle more. Not till I find some new hands in here."

Emily's spirits dropped. She'd had such hopes of making a sale. But she pushed on. "That's what the hotel manager said. But wouldn't it be fine to have a small piece, saying what kinds of work you do? Maybe a sketch of a simple outfit the women around here would like?"

Ruby gave a little snort. "What good's lookin' at what we see every day? How about a picture of a fancy gown from the city?"

"Land sakes, where'd a body wear something fancy in Wylder?" Mrs. Lowery finished unlacing the back of the green dress so Ruby could step out.

"Well," Ruby glanced at the reflection of the widow's lowered head, then threw a mischievous smile at Emily. "Them kinds of outfits must be pretty hard to make."

Mrs. Lowery blew out a dismissive breath that whistled through her front teeth. "You saying I can't sew that fancy? I can sew anything, and all my help can too."

She glared at Emily. "Go on, print a sketch of a fancy gown and put my name under it. I'll trade you— half off one of your orders for the ad."

Emily didn't know whether to laugh or groan. She'd nabbed another ad, but not with the money she needed to pay bills. Still, a first step was a first step. "Done," she said. "You'll be pleased. And who knows, when the ladies see your ad, maybe one of them would like to work for you."

The dressmaker straightened, her gaze assessing. "You mean, advertise for help?"

Emily snapped her mouth closed. Why not? She could start a new column, maybe once a month. Businesses could advertise for workers. People could see what jobs were available in town without having to visit every establishment.

"A wonderful idea, Mrs. Lowery. Thank you for the suggestion."

The woman lifted her chin a little and managed a tight smile. "Weren't nothing."

Emily jotted a few sentences in her notebook, then looked up. Ruby had donned her regular attire by then and stood before the mirror, straightening her hair.

"Oh, my," Emily said, as if just noticing. "You've hurt your mouth. That must be painful." In the mirror, the other woman exchanged a glance with Mrs. Lowery.

"I was clumsy yesterday is all. It'll be fine." Obviously, she wasn't going to mention the details in front the newcomer to town. She nodded to both, then left.

"Do many of the girls at the Social Club have clumsy accidents?" Emily fought to keep her voice level. The thought of violence to any woman made her ill.

Mrs. Lowery frowned at her. "Don't be getting any ideas about writing stuff in your newspaper, now. Some things are best left to work out on their own."

"Very true." Emily tapped her notebook on her wrist. "You know, someone mentioned earlier that a Mr. Holden has entered the race for mayor. That's good for Wylder voters, having a choice. Where does Mr. Holden work?"

"Horace's been here for years," Mrs. Lowery said. "Works down at the telegraph office. You better go now, or I'll never get them dresses of yours done."

"I'll bring the ad by later in the week for your approval then," Emily said. She smiled. "Thank you." She carried Mrs. Lowery's frown with her when she left.

Her luck in selling ads didn't improve as the afternoon wore on. Jake's Place, the bank, and the livery declined, although the Mercantile agreed to a small placement. After she'd finished at the Mercantile, she headed back to the office.

Charlie had stored all the supplies and was arranging the individual letters into the groupings he was used to. She tossed the notebook on the desk and went to the back.

"It looks like my first issue will be small. Did you include any half sheets of paper?"

"Yep. Your brother thought you might want 'em."

Bless David for knowing her—and probably Wylder too—so well. "How soon can we go to press?'

"Well, now, Miss Emily, soon's I get these letters straightened out, we can think about it."

"Then I'll start on the articles. If you have time after you finish there, would you run down to the telegraph office. Tell them to save the news reports." She stopped short. Horace Holden worked at the telegraph office. Perhaps she could go. No, she'd save that for later. She wanted to put her ideas down right now, while they were fresh in her mind.

At home later, Emily tried to read more back issues, while kitty imagined it to be a game of swat-the-paper. The small mantel clock in the living room struck eleven p.m. when she turned out the last oil lamp. She lay in bed, as wide awake as the still-lively town, whose raucous sounds drifted through the open window.

Good grief, talk about a Babe in the Woods. She'd come tripping into Wylder as naïve as a newborn. Well, she wouldn't back down. Tomorrow, she promised herself, she'd do better with finding news.

Chapter 18

Morgan pulled off his damp kerchief and mopped the back of his neck. Damn heat. He'd heard Wyoming's sun was a tepid shadow of its brother down Texas way. But for the last couple of days, the rays beat down on his head and back like a branding iron. Laramie had to be near.

He'd tracked his prey from the stockyard in Cheyenne. Foster hadn't thought to mention Bob Roberts sold cattle regularly there. Morgan had traveled over rocks, through gullies, and up hills, crossing flat, dry spurts and the occasional expanse of grassland. In the shrinking town of Buford, he'd found a bartender who remembered a fast draw fella carrying a wad of paper money. "Marshal ran him outta town when he near kilt a miner over a dance hall girl. Mona was her name."

"This Mona work here?" Morgan asked.

"Naw," came the answer. "She up and married that there miner, and they left for parts unknown. If'n you want a girl, I kin recommend a couple."

"I better be on my way." Morgan tossed a coin on the bar. "Thanks for the information."

The bartender snatched the money and shoved it in his pocket. "Might try Laramie," he called after Morgan. "I recollect him talking about the fort there. Got a brother or a uncle or somebody in the Army."

The tip felt right to Morgan, as long as Bobby Bullseye was the man he suspected he sought. Dan McKay had enlisted in the Union Army during the war. If he came through the fighting alive, he might well be making a career of it.

From Buford, Morgan pushed northwest. He came upon a few deserted campfires with cold and scattered ashes. No way of knowing who left them. As he rode the trail, mostly seeing no one and nothing but an animal here and there, he thought. About why Eli Foster had hired him. About why he'd been given the thinly veiled order to kill a man. Which he had no intention of doing.

It all didn't make sense. He wouldn't push the thoughts—they'd settle to a pattern eventually. Usually did.

Foster had hinted that Bobby might have been in on the Olsen raid, even killed Sven. But how could that be possible? Unless Bobby had learned to fly. Otherwise, the man couldn't be north of Wylder shooting Olsen, over in Cheyenne selling cattle, or up in Laramie also selling cattle, all pretty much at the same time.

It took more than a day to ride from Wylder or Cheyenne clear up to Laramie. Unless a body caught the train. But his questions to the Cheyenne ticket clerk hadn't turned up a passenger resembling the description Foster provided.

The boss hadn't been honest with him. From what Foster said about Bobby, Morgan had a good idea the two were a lot closer than Foster'd let on. Sounded like Foster had a special interest in this man, more than just as a rustler. Personal like. Something sure as hell smelled off about the whole thing.

In between turning the mystery of Foster over in his mind, Morgan thought about the woman. The lady. Emily. Memory of that incendiary kiss they'd shared before he left still had the power to make him shift in the saddle. Couldn't deny he wanted her.

And he liked her. A surprise. She was a quirky mix of high class and down to earth. At first he'd pegged her as snooty and entitled, as out of place in the West as teats on a bull. Wasn't long, though, before he found her stubborn and determined, intent on getting that tiny newspaper going. And kind as hell.

Most females would have had hysterics if they traveled hundreds of miles to a strange place only to discover the only person they knew there had disappeared. To find herself abandoned in a way of life she'd never seen before.

Not her. She was going to by-God forge ahead if it killed her. Or left bleeding boils on her hands and ink stains on her pretty ruffled skirt. The picture she'd made sitting askew in the rig that day he came upon her driving back from Cheyenne made him chuckle. The way she'd laughed at herself. That was the moment he'd known she was special. Not just a pretty and indulged female, but a woman of depth and humor.

She'd been disappointed, though, that her tea had scattered. He wondered if she even knew how to start a fire for tea water. He should have asked when he drove her home. Surely someone in town had given her a hand—and advice.

He found himself imagining how she'd greet him when he returned. Would she have reconsidered the embrace they'd shared? Her cheeks had flushed pink, and her breathing become ragged. She'd trembled against him. He could swear his arms throbbed with the memory of her soft body. And there went other parts of his body, throbbing once more. He shifted to rearrange himself in the saddle.

A dry breeze tugged at the damp scarf between his fingers. He closed his eyes and raised his face. For an instant, he imagined he caught a faint, sweet fragrance, *her* fragrance. He removed his hat for the breeze to caress his soaked hair. Despite the heated air, he felt refreshed.

Ahead, a movement caught his eye. Not a rider. Train, off to the right. Sure enough, there came the whistle. Squinting, he made out objects set against the horizon. Laramie. A sense of anticipation rushed in his veins as he pushed on across the landscape.

Once he reached town, Morgan settled his horse in the livery, found a barber's where he got a shave and, wonder of wonders in the back behind a curtain, a bath. The water was heated in a barrel set in the sun, but no matter. The lukewarm temperature felt like pure bliss.

A good rubdown sounded mighty fine to him too. And maybe a woman. Slake all that excess tension built up over the last days. Better do so here. He sure as hell didn't want to visit the Wylder Social Club, or an upstairs room at one of the saloons. He cringed at the thought of bedding a woman in his hometown. *Her* hometown. Emily.

A woman would have to wait till he finished business, though.

After finding a hotel and downing a quick bite, he stopped by the nearest bar for a drink and some indirect questions. No luck. Weariness set in—that drink had been a mistake—so he headed back to his room to sleep.

The next morning, he said hello to Brag and arranged to hire a mount for the day. First stop, the fort. And wouldn't you know it. Corporal Dan McKay was out with an escort detail and not soon expected back.

The rest of the day, Morgan scouted the town but turned up no trace of the man he trailed. Inexorably, his gaze returned to the distant white-capped mountains. His gut bunched in anticipation. Soon he might be heading that way, across the mountains. What would his life be like then? A new start, where he wasn't likely to run into anyone from his previous life. Either one of them.

In the near distance, he could make out some good-sized rock formations. He narrowed his eyes—a half day's ride, maybe more. Might be a good place to poke around. The Bobby of his memory shied away from towns for sleeping. At least, he had all those years ago. Otherwise, the landscape close by was flat and sparse as far as hiding spots went.

Riding back into town, he spied a small saloon down a side street he'd missed earlier. He could use a drink before looking for supper. The interior was dim, the atmosphere heavy with smoke from cigars and roll-your-owns. He stopped at the splintered wooden bar and tossed down two bits. "Whiskey."

The bartender sauntered over, tall, burley, more hair on his chin than his head. He plucked up the coin, then grabbed a bottle, poured out, and set the bottle beside the full glass.

"Just get in?" The question was conversational enough, but it came wrapped in a challenging tone.

Morgan nodded. "Looking for a friend."

The other man snorted. "Ain't we all?"

Morgan raised the glass in a salute and downed the contents.

The bartender swabbed the wood, intent on polishing out a knife scar. He flicked a glance to the end of the bar, just as a girl slid in beside Morgan. "Bring my companion a glass," Morgan said.

"Thanks," she said. "Want to come sit with me?"

"I'm passing through is all. Needed to wet my throat." He handed her the half-full bottle. "For your trouble."

She slid her hand around his elbow and tugged. Her smile was a closed-mouth curve. "You'll want to come sit with me."

The way she said that, Morgan agreed. The girl percolated with tension. She led him to a table against the back wall, plopped the bottle down, and motioned to a chair. She pulled one close.

"Fellow I know thinks he might'a recognized you…if you hail from Missouri and you're called Dan. Dan Morgan."

God a'mighty. How many years since he'd heard that name? "Where is this friend of yours?"

He glanced around. No one familiar. In spite of the heat in the room, cold sweat beaded his forehead.

"He had to leave right quick. Went to the outhouse."

"Whiskey'll do that to a man. Where is this privy?"

She looked toward the nearby corner, and he spotted the dim outline of a door. He rose.

"Thanks. Keep the bottle."

"Intend to."

Morgan eased out the narrow door to the back. Late twilight provided reasonable vision. No narrow little building in sight, but he did spy a lean-to stacked with firewood. As he moved toward it, a figure stepped forward into the faint glow.

Chapter 19

"Rob McKay. I thought it must be you."

"Little Danny Morgan. How the hell are ya? Damn, not so little these days."

"Been a hell of a lot of years, Rob. You've grown some yourself. What in God's name you doing all the way out here?"

Rob ignored the question. "You lookin' for me?"

"I'm looking for Bobby Bullseye. Last time I heard that name, you'd just won the county turkey shoot. All the kids were calling you that."

Rob chuckled. "Long time ago, that was. Good times." He upended a chunk of wood and sat. "I could ask you the same thing. What in hell you doing way up in Wyoming?" He jerked his head around. "You ain't...you never...you workin' for Foster? Don't tell me you finally learned to shoot a gun?" His voice turned solemn. "Guess you had cause, didn't you?"

Morgan grabbed his own hunk of wood for a seat. "I learned to get by. After the war, I worked down Texas way a few years, then scouted on one or two cattle drives north."

"Ever get back?"

Morgan knew he meant the Missouri Border. "Close I ever got was Wichita, with a cattle drive once. That was far enough. Brought back too much."

Both men sat lost in memories for a silent while.

Then Rob gave a short laugh. "You know that turkey shoot I won? Never did get to eat that bird. Jayhawkers attacked afore Ma got around to cooking it."

"After that night, I heard you joined a bunch around Westport?"

"Went on a few raids," Rob admitted. "Once the war ended, I rode with some friends for a while. Didn't take to robbin' banks and such, so I parted ways with 'em."

"Rough life, that," Morgan agreed.

"Short life."

Silence fell again while the two rolled a cigarette each. Then Morgan said, "Eli Foster sent me to find you. He says you've been stealing cattle from him and other ranchers around Wylder, killed one of the ranchers. Then had the nerve to sell one of the stolen marked bulls in Cheyenne. He took it as an affront."

"Just like I meant it. You know, he's looking to make a name and a fortune for himself," Rob added.

"I wondered if he didn't fancy a political career," Morgan said. "Tell me how you ended up in Foster's crosshairs."

"I'll tell you what I know. 'Bout two, three years ago, the Union Pacific sent him to Wylder. On his way out from the East, we happened to share a hand of poker in some railroad saloon in Nebraska. Got to talkin', and he told me to look him up if I ever found myself around Cheyenne. To make a long story short, in a few months, I went to work for him on the ranch he got outside Wylder. At first, it was the usual. Ridin' herd on cattle, regular chores around the place.

"One night he called me and another hand in, offered us a deal. Now and then, we'd pick up a few unbranded cows that might be strayin' around, slap a Bar F on them, and he'd see we got a little extra in our monthly wages. But then he comes up with this crazy idea. We'd take as many head as we could at a time, branded or no. When they came from the influential ranchers, especially those with an 'in' at the Territory Legislature, he'd give 'em back."

"Let me guess," Morgan said while Rob finished his smoke and built a new one.

"Him and some of the boys from the ranch would volunteer to help the sheriff find the stock. You'd arrange where to stash the cattle until Eli gave the word, usually in a couple of days. Then you'd hand them over to him and he'd return them, looking like a hero."

Rob snorted. "You got it. Sometimes he'd tell the sheriff him and the boys fought off the rustlers, once he said one of his boys spotted 'em corralled up in some rocks. Once in a while we'd keep one or two head for ourselves."

Morgan listened with a shake of his head. He muttered, "Son of a… Sometimes I hate being right."

"Good plan, huh? Nobody got hurt, I picked up a few extra dollars, had room and board and a monthly paycheck on top of that. We never hit too often, so folks wouldn't get suspicious."

"What changed?"

"Not sure. He'd take these trips for three, four weeks back East. Said he was on company business. Well, the last time he come back from one of them trips, the rules changed. We were to hit some of the small ranches, but these cattle wouldn't be found. I guess he'd got to trust my work, because he told me to drive 'em south into Colorado. Sometimes I got rid of a few at the mining camps. Sometimes I went north. Depended. I'd get a split of the proceeds."

This, too, matched what Morgan had surmised from his short time with Foster. "And when those small ranchers couldn't make it after that, they'd sell. Foster showed up with the cash to buy them out and help them leave. He's got the reputation as something of a savior. I believe I know just which ones were targeted. The ones with land along with railroad right of way."

"That's what I figured too," Rob said. "Took me awhile to parse it out, but yeah. I ain't sayin' I reformed in a flash of lightnin', but one night we hit nothin' but a farm—they didn't have cattle, nothin.' And damned if Ray didn't set the house afire. Little ones runnin' out, cryin'."

Rob leaned forward and rested his forearms on his knees. "I swear, Dan, it was like that night the Jayhawkers burned our place. One of those kids could 'a been me."

Or Morgan, the next year. A shiver raked his spine.

Again silence fell. A beam of lamplight faded through the small window high on the saloon wall. The back door swung open, and the girl from earlier peeked around.

"You all right out here, Bobby? Want something to drink?"

"Naw, honey. We're fine. Just catchin' up."

She ducked back inside.

"So why did you quit Foster?"

"Well, a couple of days after that farmer was burned out, I went to his office by the station and asked him for my money. He'd been keepin' it in his safe so there'd be no question about where a cowhand got so much cash to deposit in a bank. Told him I'd be movin' on, wanted to see California before I got much older. He said he didn't recall havin' any money of mine. But if I couldn't do the job I'd been hired for, I could head anywhere I wanted. Couldn't let him get away with that, could I?"

"So you hung around, snatching a few head here and there?"

Rob barked a genuine laugh. "Drove him mad! I'd wait 'till Ray and the crew made a raid, then grab a few from them. I needed to get my money back, plus I owed the bastard."

"Maybe more than you know. Word is, you shot and killed Sven Olsen a week or so ago. In fact, you're blamed for all of it, you and your gang."

"Hell, now I got a gang? I never knew I was so famous. No wonder he's set his best against me. That's what he told me that night, you know. That I could just clear out, 'cause he'd sent for the best. Word about Morgan Dodd got around fast. Damn, never figured that was you."

"What about that partner of yours? Did you say his name was Ray? Dirty yellow hair?"

"Foreman?"

Morgan nodded.

"That's the one. Keep the eye in the back of your head open 'round him. He never liked the idea of bein' second. Not to me, and it's a damn bet not to some new shootist up from the South. He wants to be the only rooster in that barnyard."

Morgan ground out his cigarette.

"Why did you make that one mistake? Sell those

cows in Cheyenne, right under his nose?"

Rob took a last draw from his cigarette, then flicked the butt away. The glow arced out of sight. "I got to thinkin' 'bout what I told old Eli. Time to move on. I was gettin' mortally tired of the game, so I wanted him to know I was the one who'd been robbin' him, in case he'd misunderstood before."

He sighed and stood. "Look over there." He nodded toward the mountains, snowcaps winking in the moon's milky glow. "I'm headin' that way. Through the pass. New beginnin'. Join a wagon train to Oregon, I thought. They can always use an extra hand. Rob McKay, at their service."

"Not Bobby Bullseye?"

Rob faced him. "Whether you kill me here tonight or not, Bobby Bullseye's dead."

"I'm not going to kill you, Rob. Hell, maybe you'd outdraw me."

"Naw. Can't shoot the schoolmarm's boy, now can I? But Old Eli's gonna be mighty mad if you don't bring back me or my gun."

"He'll have to get over it. Like you say, Bobby Bullseye's dead. Reckon we'd best make it official here in a few days."

Rob laughed and slapped his knee. "I get to plan my own funeral. What a hoot! I'll send Sophy out to buy the coffin tomorrow."

"Will the undertaker have something he can carve the name on?"

"Reckon I can do that myself. And I got a couple of papers for you to take back, might come in handy if you want to see old Eli took up."

The silence that fell then felt easier to Morgan, and

final in a strange way.

"Why don't you come along?" Rob asked. "How 'bout it? We can both make a new go in a fresh place."

Morgan stared at the mountains. Why not? It's what he'd been planning all along, once this job ended. But his money was in Wylder's bank. And…he pictured Emily standing in the doorway of the newspaper office. His heart did a funny *ker-thump*, and his arms gave a quick twitch.

"Maybe later. I'd better clear up things here first. But thanks." Morgan could hardly make out his childhood friend in the dark, but he thrust out his hand. "I wish that Missouri boy Rob McKay a happy future as a farmer."

Chapter 20

Balancing two large mugs of coffee and a half dozen fresh biscuits on a tray, Emily gingerly stepped onto the boardwalk in front of the newspaper. The door stood open. Charlie was there already, as usual. The hour had barely passed eight, but after five days, she'd learned he liked to arrive early to get in as much work as he could before the heat of the afternoon. During which he somehow managed to cool down at the Longhorn Saloon.

She set the tray on the desk inside and removed the towel that protected the food. A fly circled breakfast, and she threw the towel back over the dishes.

"Time for a break." When he appeared, she asked, "How are things going in the back?"

"Good as can be expected," came his normal morose reply. "'Bout got the wire news set."

It was a sign of her family's influence that Daniel had managed to snag a franchise for the Associated Press. Although the AP granted one such franchise per town, the small size of the paper, coupled with the price of the service, would ordinarily have prohibited the telegraph news wire for the *Sun*. As it was, they usually received only a paragraph or two summary of different topics, but major international and national stories often merited longer versions.

"Wonderful." She smiled and gestured to the desk.

"Coffee and biscuits from the hotel. Dig in."

"Hold on, I'll fetch the jam." Charlie had a sweet tooth and kept his own quart jar of pear honey on a shelf in the bookcase. When he trotted back, he set it on the tray. "Help yourself, Miss Emily."

"I'll save my biscuit for later," she said. "Right now, that editorial needs finishing."

She took a folded sheet from her reticule and spread it open. She'd spent much too long composing her first editorial, mulling over the salutation and rejecting first one, then another, but she wanted it to hit the right note. Finally, she'd decided to skip it, to simply begin.

"For those of you whom I have yet to meet, let me introduce myself. I am Emily Martin, sister of David Martin, the owner and publisher of *The Wylder Sun*. While my brother is away on family business, I am happy to be here on his behalf. He will return as soon as possible.

Meanwhile, I look forward to talking with you and learning what you like to see in your town's newspaper. I hope to keep you ~~apprised~~ informed of topics of interest and importance to the town and the surrounding area.

As you know, I am new to Wylder. And I thank you for the warm welcome I have received.

Emily Martin"

Looking over the paragraphs, she wasn't particularly pleased with the result, but it had to do. She placed it in the wire basket on the left corner of her desk. Charlie picked up her written copy there when he was ready to set it in type.

Completing the story on the special election for mayor took longer than she'd anticipated, but she ended by promising interviews with both candidates in next week's issue. She placed the sheet of paper in the wire basket and started to rise. Stopped.

Should she add what she really wanted to say? Or should she save it for next week? Usually she refused to dither over any topic she wrote about, having researched it to the best of her ability and having considered the issue from various sides to make sure her conclusions were valid. This one she needed to consider further, but she could make a beginning. *Why not?* She sat again and took the page from the basket, then made three hash marks to show an end to the article on the election for mayor and the beginning of a separate item.

Three sentences. That should be enough for now. She read over the words and compressed her lips. *Well, we'll see.*

She jotted a headline for the piece and slid it into the basket.

****

The first issue of her *Sun* was small, a single half sheet, printed front and back like a broadsheet. Still, a great bubble of pride swelled in her chest when she held it that afternoon.

"It looks wonderful, Charlie. Thank you."

He answered with a nod. "Turned out fine, if some'at skinny."

True, but Emily hoped that once folks saw she intended to maintain her brother's schedule, they'd be more likely to share information. If they would trust her, her "being a woman and all."

How many times had she heard that in the days she'd attempted to collect news?

Tommy had volunteered to deliver individual newspapers to advertisers and a stack of ten to Mr. Wylder at the Mercantile, where customers could purchase them. Another stack went to the post office to be distributed to subscribers.

She prepared one to send to her parents and set out to the post office to mail it once Tommy returned to watch the office. Charlie accompanied her as far as the Longhorn, where he offered to treat her to a celebration glass. She thanked him kindly, but continued on her way. At the post office, she collected two letters from home, then returned to the office where the evening was quiet.

The next morning was not.

Martha, her usual waitress at breakfast, greeted her with a wide grin. "Fine *Sun* yesterday, Miss Martin. Me and Ma thought you did a bang-up job." Busy with the full dining room, she couldn't stay to talk.

When she returned with Emily's regular of coffee, eggs, and biscuits, she plunked down the plate and winked. "Don't you listen to all the grumps, none, either."

Mystified at the remark, Emily glanced around. Most diners were intent on their own food, but a few men threw her disgusted glares. What on earth had disturbed them? She finished eating and put her money beside her plate.

"What do you mean by that bit you printed about the election?" demanded Mr. Willard when she stopped by the bank on her way to the office.

"All I said was that the two candidates would be

interviewed next week. What's wrong with that?"

"Not that, the foolishness about women voting."

Oh. So that explained the sour looks she'd gotten during breakfast.

"It's not foolishness, it's territorial law," she said, her tone friendly, but matter-of-fact. "Surely the women of Wylder vote at every election."

He crossed his arms. "Not my wife. Nor will she. Voting's not a woman's job."

"You trust your wife with the wisdom to run your home and raise your children. Why not with the wisdom to see what the town needs?"

When he grumbled again, Emily bit her lips together. This wasn't the time or place to debate the issue of women's suffrage. She nodded once, murmured "Thank you," and left.

Outside, she paused to catch her breath. That was a reaction she'd not expected. Surely not every man held the same opinion. Experience should have warned her otherwise, even out here where the law supposedly said differently.

Seeing Mrs. Lowery's place on the corner reminded her. Her final new gown should be ready. Determined to recast the day's outlook to positive, she made her way to the dressmaker's. Emily had hoped to open the office by eight, Charlie having the day off. But when she entered the shop, she found two other women there, neither of whom she'd met as yet. The conversation stopped when she entered.

"There she is," Widow Lowery said, managing to sound irascible and approving at the same time. "You've sure kicked a hornet's nest with that voting story, Missy."

"If all the dark looks I've received this morning are any measure, I must have," Emily said. "I don't understand why. It's the law. The fact Wyoming Territory was forward thinking enough to give women the right to vote is one reason I wanted to come here."

"Well now, it may be the law, but not for want of trying to change it," said one of the other women. "And a lot of men in these parts haven't gotten around to seeing us women as having minds."

The woman, a lovely blonde not much more than a girl really, smiled a sweet smile and held out her hand. "I'm Pearl. Ruby said she'd met David's sister in here last week."

Emily blinked. Another Social Club employee. In an instant she returned the smile and took the girl's hand. "I'm happy to meet you, Pearl. David hasn't told me a great deal about Wylder, so it's been a pleasure seeing his friends."

The other woman stepped forward. "I'm Mary Willard. It's about time somebody challenged the way things are done around here."

A frisson of alarm wiggled through Emily's stomach. This lady couldn't be the bank manager's wife. Here she stood, talking with a Social Club worker. If he knew, he'd likely have an apoplexy.

"I don't intend to challenge anything," Emily said. "Women have the right to vote here, and being able to do so is unique and an honor. I simply wanted to encourage other ladies. I had no idea there would be such reaction to a simple statement."

"Don't you worry yourself a bit," came Mrs. Willard's firm voice. "It may be the law, but around here, the ladies haven't been much in the way of voting.

There aren't many elections, so it really hasn't mattered."

Emily listened as Mrs. Lowery related a story about a woman who'd served on a jury up north somewhere. But her mind focused on an important question—did she want to be actively involved in this problem, or did she want to avoid public exposure for herself? She wouldn't be here all that long. Besides, she wasn't a suffragette; she'd never marched or picketed. Her strength lay in her ability with the written word. As E.E. Martin, her columns in the *Kansas City Times* had generated spirited discussion.

Yet very few had known Miss Emily Martin as E.E. Martin. Randolph hadn't until she'd told him, believing that her fiancé would be proud of her.

He'd been horrified. The thought of a genteel lady from polite society writing a political opinion column was appalling, he'd said. Now that they were to wed, she must stop. If his political hopes flourished, she would be his wife and make her contribution in the way women should. From the home. He would not allow her to embarrass him by continuing to write.

Besides, ladies lacked the capacity to understand complex issues. Never mind she'd attended Stevens College—it was a woman's institution, wasn't it?

Three months later, his attitude still had the power to raise her ire, even after she'd broken the engagement.

But here in the growing town of Wylder did she want to take a visible stand? Did she want to fend off scowls for breakfast every day?

"Miss Martin." The widow's voice brought her thoughts back to the present.

"Sorry, Mrs. Lowery. I was thinking."

"The girls here were asking if you planned to have a meeting for the women of Wylder, to talk about voting?"

The two watched her with tentative expressions.

A gathering of women to discuss the election? "An excellent idea, ladies. You'll tell your friends, won't you?"

"You bet we will," said Mrs. Willard. "But be sure to have the meeting during the day."

"Well now, daytime won't be good for a lot of us working women," Mrs. Lowery said. Pearl giggled. "Of course, some working women can't be there at night."

Oh, dear. "We'll settle on a time later and let everyone know," Emily said.

After a few more excited comments about rounding up friends, the two left. Mrs. Lowery got up to fetch Emily's gown. "You should of seen your face when Mary Willard and Pearl were talking like old friends. I tell you, if that husband of hers found out, he'd bust his britches. But in here, women might as well get along or they can come back another time. Or not. Makes no difference to me."

When Mrs. Lowery handed over the new dress, she said, "Any idea where you'll hold this meeting?"

Emily recalled the room at the hotel where the town council met. "I believe I know the perfect spot. I hope you'll attend?"

The widow let out a short snort. "I got no interest in riling folks up. Not good for business."

Emily paid her bill, thinking the seamstress had just contradicted herself. She turned to go when the other woman added, "But I got a interest in the election. I'll think on it."

Chapter 21

Thanks to Martha, the dining room morning waitress, a note to reserve the hotel's meeting room for a campaign conference appeared on the clerk's book the next morning, immediately after Eli Foster and one of the town councilmen finished breakfast. The manager could be excused for assuming, incorrectly, who had asked for the space.

Cissy Standish mentioned the meeting to townswomen who stopped by her shop, and several other ladies carried the message to friends. Thus, word of the gathering circulated indirectly. As Emily collected ads for the next week, several men objected to the idea of women voting for mayor. Still a surprisingly large number purchased small notices simply naming their businesses. The few pennies for each added up.

She even managed to get a smidgen of information from the two candidates for the next issue. Although, as she wrote to her mother the night before the women's meeting, she needed to improve her interviewing technique.

...Either I'm deficient in those skills, or the men assumed that I, as a female, couldn't possibly understand problems that a growing town faces. Who do they imagine buys the supplies for meals they expect three times a day? Who do they imagine selects items for the home, for cleaning, or for planting and tending

a garden? I've yet to see a man weeding vegetables behind a house in town. And isn't the issue of educating their children one for the mothers?

I fear I shall go on and on about the unreasonable attitude of some men, so I should close for now. By the time you read this, the women's meeting for the election will be over. But if you think of it, send up a prayer for us anyway.

Love to you and Father. And if you hear from David, tell him to write me!

Your loving daughter,

Emily

Finally, the evening of the meeting arrived. Armed with her pencil, her small notebook, and a copy of the territorial law granting women the vote, Emily stood to the side of the hotel desk, waiting for others. Cissy arrived, as did Martha and an older lady Martha introduced as her mother.

Pete, the night desk clerk, watched them suspiciously. Finally he asked, "Can I do something for you ladies?"

"Yes you can," Emily said. "Please show us to the meeting room and direct any women who are looking for us to the room as well."

"Umm. Sorry, ma'am, but that room is spoken for tonight," he said. "Got a election conference going on."

"That's us," she said, brightly. "We women are discussing the election."

Pete's expression of polite regret changed to panic. "Women can't be meeting here to talk about voting. It's never been done. What'll everybody say?"

"Half of everyone—that will be women—will say it's a wonderful idea," she said. She held up the copy of the territorial law. "It's perfectly legal?"

The discussion apparently caught the attention of Mr. Diamond, who appeared from the back. By that time, several onlookers had gathered to see what the commotion was all about.

"What's the problem?" Diamond asked, folding his arms on the raised desk.

Pete and Emily spoke at once, but Diamond held up a hand. "Pete?"

"These here women want to use the meeting room to talk about voting in the election."

The manager shook his head. "Ladies, I can't allow you to gather in public like this. Your husbands, brothers, and fathers wouldn't stand for it. Now why don't you all go home where you belong? Pete, didn't I see a note that the room is spoken for already, an election conference?"

"Mr. Diamond," Emily stepped to him, "the room reservation was made for us. We are having the election conference."

Diamond raised his chin and looked over the women's heads at the men who'd gathered around. Some had come from the dining room and escorted their wives. "I'm quite sure these fine people agree that women do not congregate alone at night to discuss politics. You need to leave."

Emily turned to the small curious crowd. "And I'm sure none of you gentlemen would feel threatened if a few ladies discussed the merits of the two candidates for mayor. Would you?"

No man spoke up but one of the wives stepped forward. "You may be right, Miss Martin, that the law allows women to vote, but I'm sure I have no intention of intruding in matters best handled by men. Our world is our homes and our families."

Murmurs of "quite right" and "keep to their proper places" followed.

After she delivered her speech, the woman took her husband's arm and tugged. "Let's go, Ralph."

By the time the small crowd had dispersed, a few others had arrived for the meeting. Emily considered her options. She could march the handful of women past the indignant Pete and Mr. Diamond and occupy the meeting room. She doubted either man would evict them bodily, but the uproar would certainly create a bigger scene. Nothing would be gained by that except to satisfy her stubborn determination.

She looked at the half-dozen newcomers. No use involving them in an embarrassing to do.

"Very well, gentlemen. We will leave. Ladies, come with me, please." When the small group had gained the wooden walkway outside, Emily said, "Let's go across to the *Sun*'s office. We can have privacy there."

By the time they arrived at the office, a few other ladies had joined the group. In all, ten women, including Emily, stood around the office. The last attendee—Mrs. Lowery.

"Ladies, thank you for being here tonight. How many of you are married?" Cissy, along with Martha's mother and four others including Mary Willard, raised their hands. "Did your husbands mind your coming here tonight?" Five women said no. Mrs. Willard simply smiled.

Emily sucked in a deep breath and relaxed. "Wonderful. I hope most of the men in Wylder are as forward thinking as yours are. Now about the election. I'm new to town, so I will not pretend to be an expert on what Wylder needs, nor do I propose we make any effort to back either candidate. I simply want the women in town to be aware of their right and to exercise that right if they so choose."

"I'm for that," spoke up one lady. "Although I sure do wish we had a say in what this new mayor will do. Have you left the Mercantile and tried to cross Wylder Street to the bakery for some of Mrs. Standish's sweetbread? Especially of a Monday morning after a ranch's payday on Friday?"

A few moans wafted up. "Lordy, ye can't find a place to step for all the horse leavings," added another. "I'm Stella Waffert. My man works down at the Feed and Seed. Glad to meet ye, Miss Martin.

"It would be awful nice if the town could get someone to clean the streets a couple times a month— even once a week," she added. "Then a body wouldn't mind bringing the young ones to town once in a while."

Emily jotted in her notebook. "Excellent observation. Anyone else? Perhaps once the mayor has been selected, the ladies can present a list of suggestions for improvements."

"I like that," spoke up Martha. "A Ladies' Committee."

"For Improvements," added a mild voice from the back.

"That's a wonderful idea," Emily said.

"The newspaper said you'd have interviews with the candidates," Martha said. "Maybe you could ask them what they plan for the town."

If the men will actually talk with me. "I certainly

shall," Emily said. "Meanwhile, remind your friends that the election is two weeks from tomorrow. "

"Can we meet again next week?" asked Martha. "The Ladies' Committee?"

Emily looked at the handful of women. "Would you all like to do that?"

Murmurs made the rounds. Emily held up her notebook. "I don't know all of you yet, so would you please put your names down here? And next Monday, let's meet at my house. Do you know where it is?"

"Are you living at your brother's place?" asked Mrs. Waffert. "We know that one."

"I'm at David's, yes. Shall we meet earlier?" A few ladies conferred and nodded. "How about three o'clock. Would that give everyone time to prepare dinner?"

"You mean supper?" someone piped up.

That simple question caught Emily. This matter of language kept popping up. Perhaps the way she spoke put some people off. The word "snooty" had been whispered in her wake more than once here, and she was trying so hard to be friendly. Perhaps...

"Yes, of course, supper," she said.

"I can't come in the afternoon," spoke up the quiet young woman near the door. "Don't have anyone to watch my little one 'til my man gets home."

"Bring your child, then," Emily said. "Does anyone mind?"

To a one, the women smiled. "You just bring that sweet baby, Tilly. There'll be plenty of us to watch her," Martha's mother said.

Emily bid goodbye to each lady. She hugged Cissy, the last to leave. "Thank you, my friend. I'll see you soon."

When she was finally alone, Emily sat at her desk, feeling wrung out. She'd never anticipated such an emotional reaction. She thought back. Hadn't she? The morning she'd decided to add the item about women voting, she'd paused, unsure, before she'd written it.

Oh, she'd had an idea all right. *But I had hoped.*

Well, even when it was legal, change wasn't always simple.

After she closed up, she walked home by light of a half-moon. By the time she'd reached the corner, she was squinting to find her footing. She'd not realized how dark the alleyway was that ran behind the house. Voices sounded in the distance, and a few piano notes occasionally floated through the night.

A muffled thud caught her attention, and she instinctively slowed her pace and sharpened her hearing. There. A rustle behind her she hadn't notice before. She stopped for a better listen. Nothing. She huffed a breath. Wonderful. Now she imagined things.

But when she resumed walking, the faint sound came again.

Someone followed her.

Her first instinct was to turn and confront the culprit. That probably wouldn't be wise in this place where so few people were around. Instead, she continued, quickening her pace gradually. The house was just ahead. The back door should be unlocked. She hadn't gotten into the habit of locking any door here because the town had seemed so quiet and friendly.

The pounding of her heart interfered with her hearing, and she couldn't tell if whomever it was had gained ground—or even if he still followed. She reached the back door in three long strides, flung it open—unlocked, thank the Lord—then slammed it behind her, latching the hook in one movement. Under cover of the blackness inside, she peered from the kitchen widow.

A shadow continued down the alleyway. Her breath gushed out, and she rubbed a hand over her jittery stomach. It was likely someone who lived in a house on down the way. How foolish of her to suddenly be afraid. She blamed her unease on the uncertain mood of earlier.

Suddenly, a light, soft touch stroked Emily's ankle, and she smothered a yelp. It was followed by a high yowl from the floor.

"Oh, kitty. You nearly scared me gray. Come here, you darling." She swept the rapidly growing kitten into her arms and rubbed a cheek along its side.

In the few days she had been in residence, kitty had proven to be indoor trained and a comfortable house mate. Despite a few frayed spots on Emily's favorite chair. And a slight escapade with a parlor window drapery.

Emily set kitty on the dry sink while she lit the oil lamp, then gathered her up again. In spite of Emily's entirely reasonable conclusion as to the source of her late-night follower, she'd lock the front door as well as the back. Not that she was alarmed, but once the lock slid into place, she finally eased.

How foolish she'd been. All this turmoil had her imagining things.

Chapter 22

Early the next day, Emily knocked once then walked into Eli Foster's office.

"Good morning, Mr. Foster. I'm glad to catch you before you begin your duties for the day. I just have one or two things to ask for the election article I'm writing."

Foster had scarcely taken his seat and could hardly say he was in the middle of a project. Emily knew this, because she'd spotted him in the hotel dining room earlier and had hurried to the train station to wait for him. She had no intention of allowing him to elude her questions this time.

She sat in the chair in front of the desk. "I'm asking both candidates the same questions. You won't mind, will you?" She smiled as she opened her notebook. "Now, what are the three most important issues you believe the town faces, and what do you plan to do about them?"

He stared at her a moment before he cleared his throat and took a deep breath. From the look in his eyes, she knew he didn't intend to answer. Sure enough, he turned on his charming manner and smiled in return.

"My goodness, Miss Martin, you take a man's breath away with your energy this early in the morning. I would be most happy to help you with your little story, but today is full of obligations. Why don't we discuss your questions over dinner tonight? I'll pick you up at your home at six-thirty. How about that?"

Her little story? If Emily had been kitty, she'd hiss. "That's very kind of you, but I'm afraid our policy is not to mix business and personal matters. Interviewing a candidate while on a personal engagement with him would be unethical."

She actually nipped the side of her tongue as a reminder to watch her words. "While having dinner with you would be delightful, of course, that would have to come at some future time."

His gaze held hers for a moment, and she thought she detected admiration. Then he chuckled. "Well, now, you can't blame a man for asking such a lovely lady to share a meal with him. Frankly, I feared you would say no unless there was a good reason to accept."

The reply disarmed her. Oh, she was used to flattering words from men, especially those who sought favor with her father through her. But Foster's last sentence held a hint of self-consciousness that made her wonder.

Blast it, she would not be sweet-talked into forgetting the reason for her presence there.

"We could discuss dinner at another time. Right now, I must ask you to answer these questions."

"Very well. I see I've been outmaneuvered." He settled back into his oversized chair. "Wylder is a growing community, and we must make sure the businesses that locate here are honest and will serve the residents as a whole, not just a certain element. By that, I mean saloons and the like. Not that we want to keep them out, but it would be good to confine them to the same area of town.

"Next, we've got to see that Sheriff Hanson has

proper deputies. He's getting on in years for a lawman in a booming town, and he may retire soon. If so, we want to make sure we have a strong replacement.

"I suppose you could say I favor law and order and mean to maintain it as Wylder grows.

"The third issue is extremely important and one I'm uniquely qualified to handle, and that's business development itself."

He leaned forward and rested his arms on the desk. "Let me just say this, my dear. I have knowledge of upcoming changes that will see this area grow like never before."

Emily finished the notes, ignoring the overly familiar "my dear". "These changes…" She glanced up to find him staring at her intently, an odd light in his eyes.

"Don't ask me what they are," he said. "I'm not at liberty to disclose them at this time. But I am in a position to know they will mean unprecedented expansion in Wylder."

"That sounds exciting—and mysterious," she said. "Do these changes possibly have anything to do with the company you represent?"

He stood abruptly. "I can't tell you more. I would be the worst kind of agent to let a beautiful woman coax secrets from me."

A strange mix of emotions fought in Emily— excitement that she'd identified a potential action the railroad might take and overriding suspicion that his entire answer had been a performance.

But to impress or to mislead?

She rose. "Thank you, Mr. Foster. What you've said will be of interest to Wylder voters."

He came around the desk to open the door for her. "I hope to see more of you in the future, Miss Martin."

She gave him her business smile and nod as she left.

That proved interesting. Emily wasn't sure what to make of the man. In the few times she'd met him since she arrived, he'd been pleasant, and she'd begun to think her first impression of him had been wrong. But her observation during this interview renewed her reservations. Something definitely to be analyzed later.

Her next step, interview Horace Holden. The telegraph office was close, so she headed that way.

He welcomed her with a grunt and a "reckon I could talk to you for a bit."

Checking her notes, Emily asked him the same questions.

"The three most important issues the town faces?" Holden repeated. "Well, now, I have to say Wylder's doing right good, as is. We got a great little town here, and it's growing. I reckon we have to see that new businesses get started right and that they're protected. So the sheriff needs more help, that's for sure.

"And I reckon we better set a town curfew for folks, seeing as how the ranch hands and the soldiers on leave like to let off steam ever now and then. Don't want none of our womenfolk getting in the way of the high spirits."

Emily lifted her pencil. "Do you mean set a curfew for townspeople to stay away from the business center, or a curfew for the men letting off steam, as you put it?"

"Well, now, ma'am, those boys need a outlet, what with working so hard all week. Only natural they might get right rowdy at times. We need to keep our ladies safe away from such. Other than that, I don't see no changes needed right off. We got a great town here, and folks are happy the way it is. 'Course, if things come up, we'll take care of them when they do."

"I see." She finished writing. "One last thing. What do you think about women voting in the election?"

Silence stretched. Finally Emily looked up. His face was puckered in an all-over frown, and she knew what was coming. She took a deep breath. "Mr. Holden?"

"Well, now, it ain't gonna set too good with some folks, I reckon, but I don't see a thing wrong with ladies voting. My ma knew what was what, more times than my pa did. And my missus has a good head on her shoulders.

"She's the one told me I oughta run for mayor. She says Eli Foster's too interested in what Wylder can do for him, not what he can do for Wylder."

"That's wonderful," is all Emily permitted herself to say. She wanted to cheer in surprise. And to indulge the tiny thought that it was a pity Mrs. Holden wasn't running for mayor. Perhaps she would be interested in Emily's project.

"Thank you for your time, Mr. Holden. Will you tell your wife we'd love to have her join the next meeting of the Ladies' Committee for Voting? I'll send you a note with the time and place."

"Well, now, I bet she'd like that."

Emily was lost in thought as she walked to the *Sun* office. She couldn't quite believe what Eli Foster had said. What was the real reason he wanted to move to town and take charge as mayor? From what she'd been told, he had a large ranch—and he'd been accumulating more land, buying from the families who left. With his position secure as one of the biggest ranchers and landowners in the county, what would make him move into town?

Just how much more land *had* he picked up? She stopped before crossing Wylder Street, tapping a letter from home against her chin as a wagon loaded with feed lumbered past. Instead of stepping into the dirt road, she veered right. The Land Office should be able to provide an answer to that question.

An hour later, head ringing with numbers, Emily closed her notebook. Instead of answers, she had even more questions.

Chapter 23

The next issue of *The Wylder Sun* carried a report of her interviews with both mayoral candidates. The story had no editorial comments reflecting the opinion of the editor, no leading references to anything in the men's backgrounds outside of their plans for the town.

In addition, a few lines announced the next gathering at Emily's home of the Ladies' Committee for Voting. More ads had been collected, including a few one and two liners urging votes for favorite candidates. Emily let out a sigh of relief when Charlie signaled the issue was ready to run.

Tommy had been hired not only to deliver but to help out with the Friday publications, and he was proving to be an avid learner. He was also an excellent source of tidbits picked up from livery customers and businesses where he delivered papers.

Meanwhile, Emily began to outline a story coming together from various pieces of information—unlike Tommy's gossip—based on reports and figures she'd been assembling about Foster. The story still lacked a focus, a center for all the various facts. Lots of "whats" were piling up, but so far no "whys" had surfaced. Until then, there wasn't a real story.

All in all, the last several days had been overflowing with activity—mental and physical.

Only in odd moments did the thought of a taciturn cowboy cross her mind. Moments such as when she walked past the press a dozen times a day, stored or retrieved something from the bookcase where he'd kissed her, evenings when she worked late and occasionally imagined his voice whispering "Emily" in the shadowy office. Or at night, when she lay in bed with kitty's soft fur against her cheek and listened to the distant sounds of an open Western town—shouts, laughter, wisps of piano music, the occasional gunshot.

Or when she started her day with Cissy at the bakery.

"Something on your mind?" Cissy asked that very morning as they settled for coffee and cinnamon buns.

"Not really…well…maybe."

Cissy laughed.

"What?"

"You said 'maybe' not 'perhaps', like you used to."

Emily chuckled. "Well, *maybe* I'm trying to fit in. I didn't realize the way I spoke put people off—until someone pointed it out to me."

Cissy sipped her coffee, then put the mug on the table with a click. "I'm not talking about that. Word is you and Eli Foster had dinner not long ago."

"Oh my, word travels fast."

"What can I say? I open early, and lots of customers pass through." Cissy tilted her head and raised her brows. "Something there to report?"

"For goodness sakes, it was one meal. And he joined me at my table uninvited after I'd ordered. I didn't go with him. Frankly, I think he hoped to prove his interest in the town by showing off his house. But he only talked about it. I couldn't tour it while he's the subject of an article I'm writing."

Silence fell as they ate their cinnamon buns. Finally, Emily said, "I'm working on a story. But…" She paused to sip her coffee.

"You know you can trust me, Em. If you need to talk."

"I can't figure out why Eli wants to be mayor, why he wants to move to town when he has a huge ranch and so much land in the county. When I ask him, he always side-steps a direct answer. So I decided to see just how much land he does own."

Cissy nodded. "Heard you'd spent a good deal of time at the Land Office."

"Good heavens. Nothing goes unnoticed in Wylder, does it?"

"It's noticed and talked about," Cissy said. "This is a small town. Most folks know each other."

"And each other's business?"

"It's a small town." Cissy lifted a shoulder.

"And that's why I'm coming to love it here," Emily said. "Still, knowing that everyone knows what everyone else is doing most of the time can be disconcerting."

"Umm. Just like folks have been wondering where that new gunhand of Eli's has got off to. The one you sat with on your first day here? He drops by for pie when he's in town, but he hasn't been around for a couple of weeks or so."

Cissy didn't need to ask, her question was implicit.

"I haven't seen him. He may have moved on by now." Emily studied the handle of her coffee mug. The idea of never seeing him again sent an odd chill between her shoulder blades.

"Pity if he has. Interesting fellow. Tell me about this story you're working on."

Emily straightened and took a breath. "According to land records, Eli Foster now owns four parcels of land along the railroad right of way. And that's in addition to his own ranch. Three to the north and one to the south. All purchased within the past year. Two of the names I recognized—the Gordons' and Stone's, which I heard about.

"These acreages fall on either side of the parcels retained by Union Pacific. It looks something like a checkerboard, so the land doesn't form one giant holding. Maybe my hunch was wrong. Maybe he *is* just being a good neighbor."

She gave a frustrated laugh. "And why am I so reluctant to accept that simple explanation? It's what everyone else believes."

"Maybe not everyone," Cissy murmured.

The bakery door opened, setting off a loud clanging of the cowbell at the top.

"You're getting busy again." Emily rose. "Thank you for the talk, my friend."

"More later," Cissy said, picking up the dishes and greeting the two townswomen who entered.

Emily made her way to the post office and retrieved another letter from home. She was on her way out when she noticed the odd way the paper was folded.

David.

Her pulse jumped, and she sucked in a breath. Tucking the letter into her reticule, she set off for the house. Charlie could open the office today.

She untied the simple bonnet she'd bought at the

Mercantile. Its ribbon trim matched the new blue work dress she wore—and the straw was cooler than her usual hats.

Sinking into a chair, she carefully opened the letter and scanned the signature—yes, from David. She made her way slowly through the message—his penmanship was terrible—and when she finished, read it again. He'd been East, in New York and Washington, talking with various officials. Now he was at home in Kansas City, recovering from an accident. He couldn't say when he'd be in Wylder.

But the most important thing he had to say, he opened with, like a good newspaper reporter—*Dear Ems, Do not trust Eli Foster.*

By the time Emily finished the second reading of the letter, Eli's intentions in Wylder had become much clearer. If David's information was correct, the railroad company had made an offer to the Territory to switch the way it allocated the property along its right of way. Currently, the company retained every other parcel, leaving alternate parcels available for purchase or homestead or other kinds of distribution.

A few months ago, the company had offered to switch the parcels it retained so its ownership would run solidly along one side or the other of the tracks. The Territorial Legislature hadn't yet ruled on the proposal, but if that proposal was accepted, the implication for private land ownership was monumental.

She stood, the letter crumpled in her hand. Where had she stashed the map she'd sketched when she visited the Land Office earlier? It was her impression of the railroad extension from Cheyenne to Wylder, with ownership parcels on each side noted. Had she left it at the office?

No, she hadn't removed it. It must still be in her bag. She grabbed it and jerked open the drawstring top. Sure enough, the folded sheet of paper lay along the side. Spreading it on the kitchen table, she then smoothed the creases, careful not to smudge the pencil lines. The map looked something like a checkerboard with uneven boundaries, as she'd told Cissy.

In a few moments, she dropped into a kitchen chair, her heart pounding. Eli Foster had control of each section of land that marched with the company's holdings on the north side of the track. To the south, he held one, but it was opposite the railroad parcel on the north side.

If the company intended to swap all its northern parcels for all the southern parcels, Foster would own nearly all the land along the tracks from Wylder to Cheyenne. All except one which was owned by the company and which, she had no doubt, he could easily obtain.

Of course, as its agent, he'd likely have advance knowledge of the company's intent.

So that's why he'd been such a generous benefactor to the out-of-luck farmers this past year. But why would he want to establish residence in town and run for mayor?

More power? Or... Oh, she just didn't know enough about the area to speculate on why that might be. But if he had been devious enough to implement his plan so many months ago, Emily had no doubt he had a reason for wanting a powerful presence in Wylder.

The capital of Wyoming Territory was Cheyenne. That meant the Territorial Legislature met there. Was it in session now? When did it plan to make a decision on U.P.'s offer? She needed to find out. And that meant another trip to Cheyenne.

But it would have to wait a few days. She had to finish writing up her interview with the sheriff so Charlie could set it for this week's issue. Sheriff Hanson had definite thoughts on a curfew and on the need for deputies. As she hurried to the office, a fragment of conversation she'd overheard at lunch earlier in the week flitted through her mind.

Jake's Place had been packed. Seated at her favorite small table at the side back, she'd been close to a table of three—one man who worked at the sawmill, the clerk from the land office, and another man she'd not seen around town before. He wasn't dressed as a laborer, yet he didn't wear a suit. A manager from a business south of the tracks?

It didn't matter—what did were the few words she'd paid no attention to at the time. The stranger had said something about a lot at the far west edge of town, and the clerk had nodded. "Said he expected to be in with some papers next week," the clerk said. "And warned not to go talking it up."

"Boss said to expect a big lumber order soon," the sawmill man added.

The conversation lowered to a murmur, and she heard no more.

The words meant nothing to Emily at the time. But now they came back, accompanied by a feeling of dread sinking in her stomach like lead. Instinct, a sixth-sense—something—told her the "he" buying land on the quiet was Eli Foster.

Wonder what property on the west edge of town

they're talking about? Next time she went to the Land Office, she'd do a bit more searching. The men there were used to seeing her, so they shouldn't be suspicious. After all, wasn't she just a woman, trying to figure out who lived where around Wylder? Because she usually inquired about the families occupying the parcels, she was sure one of the officials thought she searched for single men who owned land. He usually smirked when she asked for the book of records.

She smiled at the thought and got an, "Afternoon, ma'am," from a passing soldier.

The next afternoon, Emily left the office early to prepare for the women's meeting. She stopped at the bakery for cookies, but all she could offer was water to drink. At least it came fresh and cold from the well.

Several ladies had gathered at Emily's home and were discussing logistics for election day. Most favored going to the polling place in pairs or groups, not because they feared rejection—it was the law, after all—but because for some, this would be the first time to vote and having a friend along would build confidence.

One mother had even offered to watch children for other mothers who wouldn't ordinarily be able to get away during the afternoon.

In fact, the meeting had gone so smoothly, the ladies agreed they wouldn't need to meet again. The half dozen original members had each brought a friend, and they all were throwing out ideas for recruiting other women in town for voting day when a knock interrupted the discussion.

Emily opened the door and found the two women from the Cheyenne Social Club she'd met at Mrs.

Lowery's. They stepped inside, then stopped abruptly. Ruby said, "We heard about the meetin' for women's votin'."

Pearl's soft voice added, "I never knew a woman could vote, but I want to."

A few gasps floated from the clutch of members. Mrs. Diamond, the wife of the hotel manager, jerked up from her chair. "You have no right to be here." She pulled the hem of her gown toward her feet and raised her chin at Emily. "Miss Martin, you can't possibly know where these women work. They have no business in a respectable lady's home."

Emily froze. Why hadn't she anticipated such a reaction? Had she really been so naïve to think none of the so-called "respectable" ladies would take offense at women whose occupations weren't, ah, socially accepted? She hadn't thought about it at all, she realized. In fact, it never entered her mind that these two women would attend.

Pearl dipped her head. "We'll go."

They turned toward to door and Emily said, "Wait."

She feared what she was about to do would end the infant Ladies' Committee, but she couldn't let that attitude go unchallenged. Stepping toward the original group, she said, "I understand your surprise and perhaps even your concern. Back East, your circle of acquaintances would not include each other. But, ladies, the West is a new place, a place for everyone, where we all struggle to build new lives. Who knows what each of us has had to overcome? When the territory was established and the law passed, no one stipulated that only certain women could vote. No. All can.

"Let's at least give each other a chance for this purpose alone, if nothing else. We have a duty to women coming after us—to our daughters—to show the way of equality—equal votes for men and women. And equal votes for all women."

Mrs. Diamond sniffed and glared at Emily. "I suppose I shouldn't expect any other kind of opinion from a *woman newspaper editor,* but I for one won't remain in the same room with these…"

"Oh, you don't have to worry none, Mrs. Diamond," Ruby said, her eyes dancing. "Your husband don't spend his time at the Social Club."

Mrs. Diamond's hat nearly slid from the back of her head, her nose reached so high as she swept from the house. Another two ladies trailed after. When the door latch snicked shut, Pearl added in a murmur, "But she might want to check Blossom Cherry's place of a night."

Emily blew out a breath. "Shall we fill our newcomers in on the plans so far?"

No overt insults were offered, for which Emily gave profound thanks, but conversation was markedly lighter for the next twenty minutes, until the clock chimed four.

"Time to get back to the bakery," Cissy said. "I have to get ready for the evening rush."

Saying goodbye to Emily, the others prepared to leave as well. As she picked up a last cookie, Martha asked, "Will you print a report about our meeting?"

"I think it might be good for the ladies who couldn't be here today to know what's being planned," she said. Several voices agreed. As they filed out the door, a few ladies nodded to the Social Club members.

When only Emily and the two remained, Pearl said, "Well, I never expected something like that to happen."

"What did you expect when you came?" Emily asked.

"I guess we didn't think we'd be stayin'," said Ruby. "But we're women. We have as much right to vote as any of them. That's what we wanted, right Pearl?"

"We like you, Miss Martin. You're all right, even if you are a *newspaper editor*." The two laughed at Ruby's perfect imitation of Mrs. Diamond. Emily had to smile as well.

"Thanks for lettin' us stay," Ruby said. "You always treat us right. That's why I wanted to ask if you planned to marry Eli Foster. He's been braggin' about findin' the right kind of wife for a successful politician. He's got big plans, and he likes to talk about 'em when he's had a lot to drink. But he's mean, Miss Martin. And he's sneaky."

"Oh, Ruby. I have no intention of marrying Mr. Foster or anyone," Emily said. "I came to Wylder to escape marriage. I'll not be considering it again."

"Good. Now it's time for us to get to work. Won't do for any of our guests to see us done up in gingham dresses and straw bonnets. They might think they took a wrong turn and ended up in church."

When silence finally enveloped the house, Emily collapsed into the long armchair. Kitty leaped onto her lap to rub against her hand. Emily picked her up and rubbed a cheek against the comforting soft fur. Good Lord, what had just happened? If the men knew their wives had spent half an hour with girls from the Social Club, they'd be up in arms. She lay her head against the soft chair back. And wished for a packet of headache powder.

Chapter 24

The next day passed like a thief in the night—quick and silent. But for Emily, chock-full of work. With the help of Charlie, she'd gathered more than enough ads and news to fill the front and back of their single sheet edition. Except for a three-inch slot on the front page he held for the story she'd yet to verify.

Next week, she might even be able to print a full sheet which, folded, would make four pages. She allowed herself a few minutes of satisfaction before turning her mind to that open strip on the front page. That article required a trip to Cheyenne tomorrow, Thursday.

With luck, she'd get the confirmation she needed to verify David's information about the railroad. Her curiosity about the land at the edge of Wylder would have to wait.

Tommy had become a regular part-time worker, spending some of nearly every day at the office. "You're not in trouble at the livery, are you?" Emily asked one morning.

"Naw. They hired Joey too. When we don't gots enough work for us both, I help up here."

"You're a good friend."

"Ahh." The boy's face bloomed crimson, his freckles tiny brown stains. "Joey needs the money. He gots his ma and sisters at home. I just got Ma and me."

Nevertheless, Emily made sure Tommy received payment each week.

He arrived at the office at eight a.m., driving the gig Emily had hired for the day. "You sure you don't want me to come along?" he asked. "You could use a man on the trip."

An image of tall dark-haired-gray-eyed ruggedness popped into her mind. Yes, she could use a special man along. Pity he wasn't available. Where had he got to? But she felt certain she'd face no problems. Nothing had happened to convince her that she'd be in any danger on the ride.

"You'd be bored, waiting around for me all day. And don't forget, this is Thursday, preliminary set up day. Charlie might even let you put an ad together all by yourself."

His eyes sparked, and he gave a quick grin. "I could do that?"

Emily almost regretted refusing his offer later as the gig bounced along the rutted road. She didn't recall the ride being nearly as rough when Morgan Dodd drove. He'd been on her mind often during the days— and nights. He was unlike any man she'd ever known. Reticent, but always alert, with restlessness boiling just under the surface. Energy waved from him. A different kind of energy from Randolph's. Randolph was driven to succeed, to prove himself better, smarter, shrewder than other lawyers. He intended a career in politics, and woe to any who stood in his way.

That almost frantic intensity wasn't what she felt around Morgan. He didn't need to prove himself. Unconscious confidence showed in his every gesture. No preening, no chest-pounding. Sometimes he seemed almost regretful when he spoke about his work. No, not regretful—resigned.

Something troubled him deeply. If only they'd had more time together, perhaps—*maybe*—he would have confided in her.

Silly girl. What makes you think that?

Their few times together hadn't included any soul-searching conversations.

Just one soul-searing kiss.

She'd relived that kiss many times over the days, and again she became lost in the sensations, the unexpected yearnings it triggered. Recalling those moments, her breath quickened, her cheeks warmed, her breasts throbbed. She scooted around on the poorly padded seat to relieve an unusual tingling in her lower body.

The movement must have traveled through the reins because the horse leaped forward, nearly jerking her off the seat. It took a few minutes to bring the mare under control and by that time, she'd gotten her unruly body under control as well.

She chuckled. What in the world possessed her to moon over a man like Morgan Dodd? A wandering cowboy, drifting from job to job across the West.

Must be the lure of the unknown. That was it. Her imagination had been caught by a kind of person she'd never met. He *was* a lure, a handsome, appealing, masculine lure she had to overcome. He'd been gone nearly two weeks, now. Likely wandered on to the next job, God only knew where. Wasn't there an old folk song about a wandering man never settling down?

Her thoughts were broken by the sight of travelers coming toward her. When had the road widened? She'd been so lost in thought, she'd missed the evidence that Cheyenne lay just ahead. Good grief, she'd daydreamed the entire trip.

Heading for the nearest livery, she intended to water her tired mare and get directions to the Territorial capitol. When she finally made it to the building where the legislature met, it was to discover it wasn't sitting at all that week.

The clerk at a desk outside the large room where members usually gathered looked her over then shrugged. "Don't know when they'll decide on anything about the railroad."

His dismissive tone said he wouldn't tell her if he did.

"But the legislature is considering a Union Pacific offer regarding the exchange of land parcels, isn't it?"

The man shifted his eyes and made a quick stroke of his goatee. He knew something, blast him. She added, "That's what a friend told me. He just came back from New York."

"What's a woman want to know for, anyhow?" He shot to his feet, a short journey since Emily could still gaze down at his face.

"Maybe I'm interested in buying a farm."

An insulting sneer accompanied his, "Sure, you're a farmer." He stepped from behind the desk and said, "You got questions about the railroad, ask down to their offices. It's my lunch time."

Disgusted, Emily crossed her arms and stared at the clerk as he headed to the steps. She'd bet her new hat the clerk would have given out more information if she'd been a man. Why was a female always treated as if she hadn't a brain in her head?

On the off chance the *Cheyenne Leader*'s editor might be talkative, she drove to the office. Not in, of course.

She had untied the reins at the hitching rail when her stomach growled so loudly, the mare turned a curious eye her way. Nearly one o'clock and breakfast had been at seven-thirty. Retying the reins, she navigated the busy street, stepping carefully to the other side toward the café she'd visited her first trip here.

The wooden walk lay a step away when she heard a low, rough voice. "Careful, ma'am. Someone might ride you down."

Her foolish heart flipped, and a tingle skipped down her spine. She raised her head to find Morgan Dodd eyeing her from the back of his gelding. He thumbed back the brim of his hat and leaned his crossed arms on the pommel. One corner of his mouth curled up in a slow, weary smile.

Weary. That described his whole appearance. His hair hung ragged around his ears, several-days' growth of beard covered his cheeks and chin. He looked tired and dangerous and way too appealing. She drew in a slow breath, fearful her pounding pulse could be heard above the racket of the freight wagon lumbering past. "Mr. Dodd. A surprise to see you. I'm just going for lunch. Would you care to join me?"

Blast, her voice sounded thin as skimmed milk. Her cheeks warmed. Had she just invited him to lunch? Her dawning embarrassment evaporated when he swung from the saddle and tied his horse to the hitching rail.

Without a word, he placed his hand under her elbow as they stepped onto the walkway. Inside, the lunch rush had thinned, so they easily found a table. He held her chair, then took off his hat and tossed it on an empty seat beside him.

A waitress appeared before either could speak, and the next few moments were spent deciding on their orders. Finally, concentrating on the rim of the coffee cup she brought to her mouth, Emily said, "Have you been traveling?"

"Miss me?" he murmured, drawing her gaze to his face. Creases dug the skin from his hairline to the corners of his twinkling eyes.

The sip of coffee went down the wrong way and she choked. She finally managed to sputter, "Not at all. Cissy—Mrs. Standish—at the bakery mentioned she'd not seen you for a few days."

He emptied his own cup and sighed. "Missed good coffee."

Emily considered this coffee barely counted as adequate, but she nodded.

He settled against the chair back and caught her gaze. "I've been on a job."

She waited for him to say more, but he simply studied her. Finally, he said, "What brings you to Cheyenne?"

"I'd hoped to talk with members of the Territorial Legislature, but they're not in session right now."

Their food appeared then, steak and eggs and apple pie. They ate in silence for a few minutes before she asked, "Are you going to Wylder?"

Morgan nodded. "But not now. I got a couple of things to wind up here first."

Disappointment made the food set heavy in her stomach. She'd rather hoped he would drive back with her. Foolish girl. Who knew what kind of job he had to complete? And why on earth would such a man want to bump fifteen miles in a tiny gig. With a woman who'd lost all her small talk today.

"You'll go back to the ranch later?"

"Yes, ma'am. I still work for Eli Foster, and I will report to him."

Emily opened her reticule beneath the table and drew out her coin purse. Slipping payment for her meal beside the plate, she rose and slid her pie across the table. "I hope you don't mind taking this. I couldn't eat another bite right now."

"I never turn down a taste of something sweet," he said, positioning her saucer next to his. Then he glanced up, his gray eyes smoky, intent, as if he spoke of something besides pie. She caught her breath, and again her cheeks burned, but she couldn't look away.

After what seemed like minutes, but likely was only a second or two, she cleared her throat and managed a bright smile. "It's probably not as good as Cissy's pie."

"Hmm. I'll let you know what I think."

Ears ringing with nerves, she nodded. "Goodbye."

She nearly stumbled over her own feet as she rushed to the door.

All the way back to Wylder, Emily replayed their conversation in her mind. And each time, she came away with the same impression. Morgan Dodd had flirted with her. Her heart did a dangerous jig. Dangerous, because she had liked it. Had wanted more. Had wanted to reach across the table, touch his lips, test the texture of that beard—rough or soft?

She thought it might very well reflect the man who wore it—rough on the outside, but soft—so soft—beneath.

Chapter 25

Morgan took a long time to finish lunch. He had a lot to think about. Not what he'd tell Foster. He'd worked that out on the long, dreary ride from Laramie. He'd been gone longer than he'd wanted, but what with the folks he'd had to see and documents to gather, the delay had been worth it.

He'd traveled a good swatch of countryside on this trip. What he'd seen, he liked. Oh, he'd been warned aplenty about the winters, about the danger of rough cold on the cattle, the short growing season for some crops.

But he didn't want an empire, just a place big enough for a wife and family to make a comfortable home. A loving home. Once he'd have laughed at the thought he might ever find the kind of contentment and companionship and, yes, love, his parents had known. He might have laughed at the thought he could ever find a woman who'd last a lifetime with him.

There was Jobeth, god-a many years ago. He'd been a kid, then, right after the war. She had stuck for a few months, until a better offer from a wealthier man came along. The last Morgan heard, she'd married that man—and buried him.

But someone like Emily Martin, now. She was a stayer, if he read her right. Honest, sincere, determined. Hell, every time he saw her, she'd overcome another hurdle in making a home in Wylder.

The way she blushed. He chuckled. He liked making her cheeks bloom that pretty pink. And what an armful.

He would not go there again. Too damn much of his journey had been haunted with thoughts and daydreams of one Miss Emily Martin. She wasn't for a wanderer like him. A shootist like him. Thank God he wasn't known as a fast draw, or wannabes would track him down for a chance to prove themselves. No, he wasn't the fastest, but he was efficient. Deadly accurate, deadly efficient. That's all he needed to be. Even so, what lady would want to tie herself to a man like that?

No, his dreams were just that—air dreams. He had no need to scout the land hereabouts. California was where he'd head come spring. Maybe look up Rob in Oregon before going south. The future was his to make, and he needed no ties. He'd leave, just as soon as he talked with authorities here in Cheyenne.

He paid for his meal and headed outside, his body hard from thinking of Emily. He'd been stiff for much of the distance he rode, thinking of how she felt against him for their searing kiss that day at the newspaper office. Time he found a little relief.

After a bath, a haircut, and a shave, he'd visit a couple of offices. Then he'd search out the willing blonde he'd bedded the night the cattle drive got in. If he could remember her name. Something with a C.

He finally ran her to ground at the Sidewinder Saloon. It was shortly before midnight, and she was still free. Or free again. Morgan didn't know. Cora, that was her name. Cora of the talented mouth. Cora was tall and blonde, with breasts like pillows. Legs that could wrap around a man's back and hips for a long, leisurely waltz or a quick, frantic jig.

Trouble was, Morgan found, he wasn't in the mood for dancing.

He sat on the side of his hotel bed—he'd preferred that to her place—and counted out bills, then added one for good measure. Worth it to him.

"Get dressed, honey," he told her gently. "I've been on horseback for days, and I'm so tired I can't— think straight."

Cora flounced over, breasts bouncing. "I can stay around for a while," she said, sliding between his knees and running her fingers through his hair. "After you rest a hour or so, might be you'll feel up to it then."

She snickered at the play on words. "You paid me enough. I can wait."

"Keep the money." He flicked her nipple, then set her away and stood. "I'll look you up the next time I'm in town. Won't be so worn out then."

He wouldn't be looking for Cora again, no matter how often he made it to Cheyenne. He'd known it before they'd even left the saloon. He shouldn't have brought her up here, feeling the way he did. Uninterested. And when she'd shimmied out of her fancy red dress with the drooping ruffles, he'd gone cold. She was clean, but she didn't have the right smell. No light flower fragrance to tickle his nose. No crisp, breezy scent coming off the fabric of her bodice.

What in hell was he doing? He didn't know if he wanted Emily Martin in his bed, but he sure as hell didn't want Cora. When he'd jollied her mood to a smile, he gave her a peck on the forehead, and after she pulled on that limp red dress, he pinched her bottom. She giggled, then waved as she closed the door.

He sucked in a deep breath and expelled it in a loud swoosh. He undressed, turned out the oil lamp, and slid between heavenly clean sheets. Through the partially open window, he caught the faint odors of cigarette smoke, stale beer, the dirt road, even an occasional whiff of the stockyard, empty now but ripe with leavings.

Sounds of Cheyenne's night life drifted in, hoofbeats, laughter, shouts, a curse now and then, staccato gunshots. Some cowboy, letting off steam.

The odors and sounds faded into echoes of emptiness.

Sleep nibbled at the edges of his mind when he realized—he wanted Emily Martin not only in his bed. Hell, he might even want her in his lonely life.

The next morning Morgan grabbed breakfast at a small café near his hotel, then gathered a rested Brag and set out for Wylder. The lonely uncertainty of last night had given way to renewed energy. And a mind clearer than he'd had for weeks.

He'd report to Eli Foster and turn in his resignation. Never mind waiting around to see the outcome of his talks yesterday. Then he'd collect his bank savings and head out. The warmth and longing he'd felt after seeing Emily Martin yesterday had cooled. There was no place in his life for a fine lady, whose soft hands were roughened only by a small callus on the middle finger of her right hand. Her writing hand.

His mouth pressed into an almost-smile as he thought of her. The strange mood of yesterday was explained by his extreme weariness and maybe a little by the foolish thoughts he'd been having about settling down, maybe near a town like Wylder, living the life he'd once thought to have. Back when he was young. Before the war.

All these past months up from Texas on the cattle drive, he'd felt a change coming, thought about seeing what turned up on the other side of the mountains. Then the odd doings around Wylder, coming at the same time, really had him spinning.

But this morning, he knew. He needed to go. Funny, now he'd decided, the urge pounded in him like the throb of a stampede. The more he thought about it, the more intense the feeling became. Urgent, restless, driving.

Coming out of his deep reverie, he realized Brag had picked up speed until he trotted right along. At this rate, Morgan's teeth would be jarred from his head before they reached noontime.

He eased the reins and rubbed a calming hand along Brag's neck. Soon he gave the signal for an easy canter, and their trip resumed its dull, quiet rhythm.

Maybe that was it. Maybe he'd been too much alone in his mind since he'd seen Rob off to Oregon. He glanced toward the mountains, at the foothills hunkered before them. And realized the sun had disappeared sometime during his long mental meanderings.

Now puffy gray clouds lay belly-up in the sky, their backs forming a flat roof hovering over the near-distance hills. No doubt about it, a storm would break by nightfall. It came faster than he thought. He'd barely made the edge of Wylder before claws of lightning ripped open the clouds, releasing torrents of rain. The wind gusted, driving restless, insistent thunder across the sky. Morgan tipped his hat, so the brim gave him a brief awning to divert the cascade of drops. With limited vision, he made his way to the livery.

Inside, he dismounted and turned Brag over to one of the workers for some serious tending. Then he stood at the door, waiting for the rain to let up.

"Howdy." Buck Standish, part owner of the livery, ambled up to join him. "Bad day to be out."

"Can't argue that," Morgan said. He knew of Standish's reputation with a gun, but he also knew the man had settled down not long ago with Cissy-of-the-fine-pies.

"I've been away for a while," he said after a few minutes of silence while the two watched the dirt street turn to mud. "Any excitement?"

"Just the ordinary," Standish said. "Regular assortment of rowdy drunks and cowboys letting off steam. Sheriff Hanson's had his cells full."

Morgan grunted. Then Standish said, "One thing's mighty interesting, though. The women in town have been talking about the mayor's election. Seems like they're planning to get out their vote. Couple of stories in the *Sun* have set 'em off."

Mention of the newspaper prodded Morgan to reposition his hat. "Trouble?"

"Nah. But it give a few of the cowhands something new to sound off about. Cissy's been to the meetings. All they talk about there is how to get the ladies to the polls. No politicking."

"Probably a good thing," Morgan said.

"I'm thinking so," Standish said. "Gotta say, I

don't much care for your boss. Not looking forward to him running the town."

"You're not alone." Morgan straightened. "Looks like it's let up out there. I better grab a bite to eat while I can. Standish, pleasure."

He'd passed the land office and made it nearly to Wylder Street when the heavens opened again. Lowering his head against the rain pellets, he charged across to the *Sun*'s office. He'd gained the wet, slippery boardwalk before realizing where his path took him. Without thought, he'd made for Emily Martin. So much for lunch.

Inside, no lamp burned against the stormy gloom. Maybe she wasn't in. He set his hat on a chair seat and called, "Anyone here?"

She peered around the side of the bookcase of steamy memory. "Oh, my. You are soaked. Come in."

She hurried forward, shaking her head. "That was a silly thing to say. Of course you're wet. Come to the back. There's a blanket and some towels."

He followed her to the corner concealed by the fabric. The emergency sleeping quarters, he recalled. "Dry off as much as you can, then wrap that warm blanket around you."

He chuckled at her flurry of concern, took the towel she handed him, and rubbed his hair dry. If she knew the weather he'd survived over the years, she'd be in a tizzy for sure. "You don't need to worry. I've been wetter than this for longer times in colder places. But thanks. I appreciate it." After a moment he called, "You alone?"

"The weekly run is finished. Tommy's delivering papers, Charlie's gone to celebrate another issue, and

I've put away supplies. So...yes. When you've finished, I have a jar of tea here. It's too cool to be hot tea and too warm to be cold tea, but it's sweetened with honey and—"

"Sounds good. I'll be right there." Tea, huh? He'd prefer a swig of strong whiskey. But she seemed full of nervous talk. The storm must have her upset. So he'd sit and drink her sweet tea and give her company till the worst passed.

As if to underscore the thought, a jagged white light flashed from outside, followed by an earth-and-newspaper-office-shaking round of thunder.

Chapter 26

Silly, silly girl. Emily shook her head at her babbling. Diarrhea of the mouth, David used to taunt when she let her nerves run away with her.

But good grief. What's a girl to do when a tall handsome male interrupts her thoughts? And soaked to the skin. His thin red cotton shirt plastered to his chest, back, and arms like wet paint, outlining every muscle, bulging and shifting as he moved. Showing that a man need not be bulky as a bare-fisted fighter to show strength. How she wanted to help him strip off that soaking shirt and scrub the moisture from his chest.

Oh dear. She pressed her hands against her warm cheeks and rushed to the desk to retrieve a clean cup, filled it with tea, then topped off her own cup. She inhaled slowly through her nose, held her breath to the count of five, then gently exhaled through her teeth.

There, calm. He'd caught her in the midst of deep mental meanderings, and the surprise of seeing in the flesh the very man who roamed those daydreams had shaken her. Like a foolish girl in the midst of her first calf-love, not a mature woman who'd broken an engagement to show her independence.

He emerged with the blanket around his shoulders over the wet shirt. "Where are you sitting?"

Oh. She'd neglected to bring the chairs. "I have a bad habit of sitting on the floor. I was over there, catching up on some back issues. Let me bring…"

She'd started for the front and the chairs, when he said, "Never mind. I'll just sit with you by the bookcase. It'll feel good, stretching my legs."

He held up a cup. "Mine?"

When she nodded, he handed her the other and went to sit. She followed, tucking her skirt around her legs before lowering herself to the floor. For a time, they sipped tea and listened to the rain. As the silence lengthened, her awareness of Morgan sharpened.

Although nowhere did their bodies touch, his warmth wrapped around her. She repressed a shiver. The not-unpleasant odor of horse and leather clung to him, along with the fresh smell of rain and a unique spicy odor that belonged to Morgan alone.

She inhaled slowly again, this time not counting the moments she held the masculine fragrance, allowing it to swirl through her nostrils, into her head, her chest. At last the breath eased out. A bit lightheaded, she leaned back against the bookcase and closed her eyes.

Aware of a rustling movement at her side, she cracked open her eyelids and saw he watched her. He'd set his cup aside.

"You must be remembering a happy time," he murmured. "The expression on your face is inviting."

She lifted her brows and widened her eyes, blinked them rapidly to bring him into focus. It didn't work because he was moving closer bit by tiny bit. When his lips closed over hers, she was breathless again.

He tasted of honeyed tea and wildness. And, surprisingly, comfort. He slid his arms around her, and she leaned into the still-damp fabric of his shirt. A shiver moved down her spine as he pulled her more fully against him.

His tongue traced the underside of her upper lip. The gentle, erotic stroke tingled all the way to her nipples. She slid her arm around his waist, pushing closer. His muffled moan vibrated against the tender contours of her mouth. Their bodies began a slow slide to the side.

Until a clank sounded. And tepid moisture hit her hand. A cup of tea had overturned.

They pulled away from each other and straightened. Morgan grabbed the blanket and mopped up the liquid.

Emily moved her own cup out of reach and tried to put her emotions to rights, along with her dress. Goodness, how had that button come undone? She secured it and cleared her throat. By that time, Morgan had resumed his place at her side. She cut him a glance to find him smiling gently. Her embarrassment eased. "Second time we've been interrupted," he said. "Someone's looking to save you from my evil clutches."

"Umm. Not so evil, maybe." She smiled and in the comfortable quiet that followed, she gathered her courage to ask something that had puzzled her. "You don't speak like a lot of people I've met here. Where did you go to school?"

Realizing that the question could be taken the wrong way, she added, "What I meant was—"

"I think I know what you mean." He drew up one knee and draped an arm across it. "I don't realize it's slipped out until someone calls me on it."

Blowing out a sigh, he leaned his head back with a thunk. "My mother was a teacher. The only one in the small town near where we lived. She made sure I had my lessons down. Guess it got pounded into my head for so long, it comes naturally. When I'm on the trail or on a job, I usually pick up the way of speaking wherever it is. But sometimes I revert without thinking."

He turned to look at her. "The way you do."

"I've been called on it a few times since I arrived. I didn't realize it made me sound stand-offish. Like I thought I was better than others."

"Bet that came from another female, didn't it?"

"As a matter of fact."

"Not all men think that way. A lot respect a woman who sounds like she might have a thought in her head. In this part of the country, smart women last longer."

"Umm." She could ask what he meant, but she really wanted to know about him. "Do you get to see your mother often?"

A strange stillness settled over him. "She died years ago."

His words and the level, aloof tone made her long to comfort him. She covered one of his hands with hers and murmured, "I'm sorry."

He turned his hand over and threaded their fingers together. "Me too."

Cooler air trailed the storm, and as steady rain replaced the violent downpour and light show, the temperature dropped. Morgan's fingers felt cold against hers, and a shiver rippled down his arms.

"Please get out of that wet shirt." She pulled at the damp cloth clinging to his skin. "The blanket you have is wet too. There's another on the bed. You'll be better off bundled in that."

"I'm fine." As if some puckish angel heard him, he sneezed. Then he said ruefully, "All right."

The sound of wet fabric peeling away from skin followed her into the cubicle where she picked up the folded blanket. Pressing it against her, she realized the front of her dress was damp from when she'd leaned against him. She smiled slightly and shook her head.

By the time she returned, he'd wrapped the first blanket around his still-wet trousers. She certainly wouldn't insist he remove them. The thought of such a thing made her face burn and her pulse jump. She shook out the dry blanket and draped it over his shoulders.

And saw the scars on his back. Odd, pitted ones on his upper side. Another place that looked like skin had been scraped off and grown back. A burn? It extended across his upper back and looked like it went all the way beneath his arms, around to his chest.

Without thinking, she started to lean forward to see where the scar led, then caught herself and sat back on her heels.

"What wrong?" he asked.

She touched a small round scar, which made him wince. "I'm sorry," she said. "Do they hurt?"

He gave a short laugh and relaxed. "Not now. You just startled me. I forget they're there."

"What are they from?" When he didn't answer, she whispered, "Were you shot?"

He pulled the wool around him and settled against the bookcase again. Finally he said, "Years ago."

"On a job?"

"No. Long time before."

"But…were you a child then? How terrible."

"I don't want to talk about it."

She scooted closer. The solid wood of the bookcase grounded her. How odd that she'd had such a reaction from the thought of his being hurt. The steady murmur of rain droning outside emphasized the silence inside until it shrunk to encompass just the two of them in a dim, shadowy bubble.

She barely heard him when he began to speak. "I was thirteen. Raiders came. They caught Dad outside the barn. Mother had just got home from school and was starting supper. I'd gone down to the creek to fish. When I heard gunshots, I hightailed it back to the house, but they were riding away. One of the stragglers saw me and got off a couple of rounds. I guess when I fell, they thought I was dead too."

"What kind of raiders? Where did you live?"

"We had a place a few miles south of Westport, not far from the Kansas border."

"Westport? Missouri?" Her breathless voice carried disbelief and fear. "You were caught in the Border Wars?"

His muscles tensed, and he gave a vague nod.

"You were shot. What happened then?" she asked in a shaky murmur.

After a while he continued. "Hours later, it was dark, a local band of Bushwhackers came along, looking for the raiders from Kansas. Guess they'd hit a couple other places to the north. Anyway, one of the men found me and took me home with him. Funny, they'd come searching to make sure the schoolmarm's family was okay."

Silence. Finally she said, "But you weren't."

"His wife nursed me for weeks. I couldn't even go

to my folks' funeral."

"What did you do after you healed?"

"Stayed with the family that took me in. Helped with their farm. Till the war was over."

Again silence fell. Then Emily asked, "The man who took you in. He was a member of a Bushwhacker group?"

"You state that mighty gently. Yes, when they thought they had to fight back."

"So...did you..."

"Did I go with him? Is that what you want to know?" His voice became stronger, challenging. "Jayhawkers killed my family. Of course I went along."

Another silence. Then he said, "And no, I never killed anyone, not to my knowledge. I didn't have much experience with guns. But after the war, I learned. Had no family, no home—it'd been claimed by someone else by then. Besides, I wanted no part of the place where Mother and Dad died. So I got on my horse and started riding."

Emily had no words when he finished. Affected by what he'd said, she was even more burdened by what he hadn't said. The pain he'd carried, the years of having no one but himself to rely on, moving from place to place, without a goal in sight. Learning to shoot, learning to deaden his gentle heart—and he'd had a gentle heart once—how had he done it?

She reached for his hand fisted on his thigh. It twitched at her touch, but she held it anyway. The other was out of reach.

"I'm sorry," she murmured again.

He cut her a glance from behind his long, thick lashes. "I don't want your pity."

The flat, dismissive tone didn't discourage her, it spurred her into action.

"A good thing, then, because I don't pity you. I am sorry for your pain and your loss, but you're a big boy now. You've made your choices."

She twisted until she faced him more fully. "What I feel for you certainly isn't pity."

Moving as quickly as her cramped position allowed, she braced her hand on his arm, lifted herself forward, and kissed him.

He snaked his arm around her waist and dragged her sideways across his lap to cradle her in the crook of his arm. Stroking her cheek with his other hand, he deepened the kiss. Emily had acted on an impulsive desire to comfort him, but when he touched her, the emotion burned away in fiery clarity. She had come to care for this stranger, this man unlike any other in her experience.

And she feared—a nervous, excited fear—that the feeling took root in her heart.

Chapter 27

Good thing he was sitting when he pulled her near, Morgan realized in a tiny, coherent corner of his mind. Else the sensation of Emily cradled in his arms would have buckled his knees. As it was, his arms ached with the need to hold her close, and closer still. She brushed her fingers across his chest where the blanket parted, and chill bumps covered him.

When he shivered, she pushed away and sat. "There's a draft," she whispered. "We should move from the floor."

A rumble lifted from his throat, and he pulled her against him again. He traced his hand from her waist, slowly over her breasts, to her throat. Curling his fingers around the side of her neck, he fit his mouth to hers.

The vivid tenderness of the moment closed around them, magnifying every touch, every taste, every fragrance. The fresh tang of rain, the mustiness of damp wood, the acridness of the metal press, and the ineffable sweetness of the woman he held. There were traces of some flowery fragrance she'd used this morning, the hominess of starch from her damp cotton bodice, and the heady whiff of arousal.

Her soft skin pulled against the roughness of his fingers, fingers more used to caressing the sensitive trigger of a gun than the sensitive silk of her throat.

Easing his tongue between her lips, he almost smiled at the blended taste of sweet honey and tangy tea. Like her. Like Emily.

Damn if his head had ever spun like this. He longed to stretch her out on the floor, to kiss every inch of her body, to make her his. Right here. Right now.

To hold her in his arms all night until unforgiving sunlight woke him to the sight of her, hair tangled around her shoulders. Tomorrow morning. And every morning for the rest of their lives.

But a long-suppressed rule poked his mind numbing with desire. This was wrong. Not *this*. Not the tenderness, not the closeness of minds, not the unbelievable feeling he'd found home here, with this woman, in this place.

Because he knew damned well that could never be. And if he allowed himself to caress her, allowed her caresses to continue, he feared he'd reach a point where no amount of good intent could stop him.

He groaned with the pain of realization. His better self—hell, he'd near forgot he had a better self—slowly lifted his lips from hers. Withdrew his seeking fingers from the smoldering depth of her stays.

Her hands halted their stroking of his chest then drew away with one last touch to the tiny mountain of his nipple.

He hissed in a sharp breath between his teeth then whispered, "Against the rules."

Drawing the blanket back up around his shoulders, she sat. "I didn't read those rules."

Emily's attempt at humor fell flat. She caught her lips between her teeth and fought to steady her breath. Her voice trembled, her hands trembled, her shoulders trembled.

Odd, because her body threatened to burst into flames at any moment. The large, hard evidence of his arousal throbbed against her hip, and she couldn't move. She wove her fingers together in her lap to keep from reaching out to touch him there.

She ought to be ashamed of herself for losing control, responding to a near stranger like that. Yet he didn't seem like a stranger. He never had, she realized. Something indefinable about him had beckoned to her from the first. As if they'd always known each other.

Oh, goodness, what a ridiculous thought. It sounded more like a comment her silly roommate at school, Lois Scott, would have made. Lois read too many foolish, romantical novels.

Still, an invisible force did seem to link the two of them. Or at least Emily to him. She had no inkling how he really felt about her.

He lifted her away from his lap and put her gently on the floor. His breath sounded ragged, and when her lowered hands brushed his front, he hissed in a breath.

…Well, except for that.

He stood and pulled on his clammy shirt. The sight gave her chills.

"Don't go out in this downpour," she said. "You can stay here, on the cot."

He shot her a narrow glance. "And where will you sleep?"

"Home is very close, you know."

She turned her back and fumbled to close the buttons of her dress. After clearing her throat, she faced him, eyes lowered. "The rain will let up in a bit, and I can dash to the house before the storm starts again."

His hands gripped her shoulders. "No. I'll spend the night at the hotel. Tomorrow we'll talk. Emily, look at me. Let me walk you home."

"No! Please. I need to go alone." Hard enough to say goodbye here. At her door, perhaps she couldn't manage it.

She turned her head, too embarrassed to face him. At his urging, she peeked up again. His hands slid down her arms to grasp her fingers. He squeezed them. "Tomorrow, when the sun is shining and we're both clear headed. We. Will. Talk. Agreed?"

"I…I…"

He enfolded her in his arms, and she leaned into the embrace, welcoming the slap of wet fabric against her face. It cooled the burn of her shame. He pressed his cheek against her hair.

"I need to talk with you." The murmur of his deep voice made her want to weep.

"We could talk now." *Please, please, please…*

"Now is not the time. We need to think with clear minds."

His solemn tone tolled in her heart. She knew what he intended to do. Let her down gently. She'd thrown herself at him, and now he thought he had to save her feelings. Yes, it hurt, but yes, it reinforced her belief in his good heart. He must know she expected nothing, that he was free to follow his dreams over the mountains. She nodded.

"Tomorrow. Ten o'clock. Here." He kissed her forehead. "Promise?"

She rose on tiptoes and kissed his cheek. "Tomorrow."

Chapter 28

As if Mother Nature took pity on them, the rain stopped. Morgan made it to his hotel room after waiting for Emily to lock the office's front door and slip out the back. He couldn't see her leave, but he imagined he heard a faint slam.

He'd stripped off his wet shirt, draped it across the foot of the metal bedstead, and was about to shuck his trousers when a firm fist threw two knocks at his door then twisted the locked knob.

He grabbed his gun and took the distance to the door in two strides. "Yeah?"

"It's Foster. Open up."

What the devil did he want on an afternoon like this? Morgan turned the key and opened the door.

Foster pushed his way in, carrying a thin leather satchel and dressed like he was heading to a fancy doings. "Finally got back, did you? Where the hell did you have to track him?" He gave a nod to the gun. "Put that damn thing away and tell me what happened."

Morgan slid the gun into its holster, crossed his arms on his chest, and pinned Foster with a level stare. "Bobby Bullseye won't be bothering you or anyone, ever again."

Foster's shoulders slumped, and he let out a breath. But his eyes glittered. "You got him? He's dead?"

"As I said, Bobby Bullseye won't threaten anyone

again."

"Proof." Foster advanced on Morgan, both hands clutched on the edges of his suit vest. "I told you to bring me something to show he was finally out of the way."

From his trousers' back pocket, Morgan pulled a folded envelope. "Got kind of damp when the storm caught me, but dry now. I reckon this will do the trick."

Foster snatched it from Morgan's fingers and tore open the flap. Dragging out the contents, he strode to the dresser and held the sheet to the oil lamp. His smile was grim, satisfied, and he looked mean as hell. "Suppose you read it?"

Morgan picked up a clean red shirt from his pack unrolled on the bed and donned it. "Did it look like I'd opened it?"

Foster flipped the envelope and examined the flap, then the name scrawled on the front. Bobby's name. In Foster's handwriting. From his expression, Foster recognized the script's slant.

"Hope it's what you want. Bobby seemed to think it was important when I took it out of his gear." And Rob had stressed the value of the contents. 'This'll convince the fool I'm dead. He'd never think I'd turn loose of this elsewise.'

Foster nodded. He put the paper to the lamp's chimney. Once a spark caught and a flame bloomed, he tossed the sheet into the metal washbasin and watched it burn. It burned slowly, edges curling in jagged black fragments, lines of writing disappearing in ash. When the small fire had consumed it completely, he splashed water on the remnants, then dumped the whole in the slop bucket.

As he stared at the remains, Morgan cleared his throat. "I've been thinking. Now this job is finished, I believe I'll pull out. Since I'm terminating my contract early, I won't ask for another payment. The advance you gave will cover my services."

That brought Foster around to face him. "Like hell you will. The job I hired you for isn't done till I say so. You're not running out on me."

"Our contract wasn't in writing, if you recall."

Foster couldn't stop a side glance at the soppy, charred remains of the one contract he had committed to paper. That would've seen him in jail if it had ever come to light. He grinned. "That's right. But I got your word, and from what I heard, that's as good as a signed paper."

Morgan straightened and raised his chin. "I'm out, and there's nothing you can do about it."

****

Eli faced Morgan Dodd. Confrontation wasn't high on Foster's list of preferred activities. Hell, that's why he hired men like Dodd and Ray and that damned Bobby. He could call Ray. Ray would take care of Dodd without a bonus at all. The way his foreman hated Dodd, he might even pay Foster for the pleasure. If he didn't do it himself. He patted his coat pocket where the fancy derringer hid.

But not yet. He had one last use for Dodd before turning him loose.

"You know." He brushed off his affable tone and managed a smug smile. "You might be right. I might not need your gun, here on out. I'm so close to my goal, I can smell it like that burnt paper. Tell you what. One last job tonight. I'll pay you another third, and you can clear the pass before snow sets in."

"Mind telling me what that goal is?"

Why not? He'd be mayor of Wylder, in a position to profit from the railroad's anticipated expansion west from here, and from the thousands of acres he'd own once the land swap was approved. From then on, no one could stop him.

"I figure I'll serve as the mayor for a term, then shoot for a seat in the Territorial Legislature. After that, with my contacts back East, maybe even a seat in Washington as territory representative."

His big plans didn't seem to impress Dodd at all. The damned gunman had the nerve to cross his arms and lean back against the foot of the bed. Eli couldn't resist stab of triumph. He'd make any promise he liked—wouldn't be carried out.

He reckoned he'd call on Ray after all. Once Dodd finished up, collected his cash, and set out, Ray could tail him, see he didn't make it anywhere he might let his dangerous knowledge slip.

Why hadn't he thought of that earlier?

Dodd was looking impatient.

"What?"

"I said what's this last job you want done?"

Eli set his leather letter case on the mattress, untied it, and jerked out the latest issue of *The Wylder Sun*. He tossed it at Dodd, who grabbed it in midair. "Look at the front page. That column right in the middle."

As the other man read, Eli's mind followed the words he'd committed to memory.

What Is Union Pacific Proposing?

"The *Sun* has learned that the Wyoming Territorial Legislature, meeting in Cheyenne, is considering a land offer from Union Pacific Railroad. A correspondent has told this editor that the offer would mean increased development for Wylder. The nature of the proposal has not been made known to the public. This editor could not reach a member of the legislature for comment."

Dodd looked over the top of the page. "So?"

"Five people already asked about the story, just since it was printed today. There's a meeting at the school later about the election coming up. All those people will have questions. I don't need this kind of bull stirring up more."

He snatched the paper, shoved it in his bag, then took a long breath. Had to calm down. Wouldn't do for folks to see him in a temper. "Tonight while the meeting is going on, I want you to make sure the newspaper can't print anything else that will make me look bad."

"Somebody already tried that, about the time I got into town. Tore everything up good."

"Not good enough. But if you don't think you're up to it, I'll call on Ray." If only he'd given the task to his foreman the first time. He'd told a couple of hands to put the place out of commission, right after that nosey editor went running. They didn't have a brain between them. "Who would have thought a woman would show up to stir the fire again? That's one damned family that ought to be dealt with."

"I thought you had your eye on courting her," Dodd said. "That's the word around the bunkhouse."

Eli pictured the fine Miss Emily in his mind and sneered. "She should have made a perfect wife for a man with a political future. But she's too damned opinionated, too damned smart for her own good. A real lady knows when to smile and when to keep her mouth shut."

An odd stillness fell over Dodd, one Eli couldn't figure. But he could feel the tension, all right. Of course. The newspaper lady. "Ray said you'd dropped by the *Sun* a time or two. You got your eye on her?"

"I figure she's not for me, neither. But that doesn't mean I'll hurt her."

Eli snorted. "I'm betting she'll be at the meeting to see what mischief she's stirred. Just take care of the damned press. And this time, make sure it's destroyed proper, not just taken apart. If the wood's not too wet, think about a little fire."

Dodd continued to stare. Finally he said, "What's so urgent that it has to be done tonight? We could wait a few days."

Why in hell did every nobody with a gun try to think? He'd like to get rid of the upstart himself. The derringer in his pocket whispered to him. No, that's what he had Ray for. Ray was the one smart hire he'd made in the last three years. He should have seen it before. A man with ambitions and no qualms about how he achieved them.

"I told you before, Dodd. Can't have any more stories like this coming out before the election. Who knows what the she-dog will print next week? Won't be time to head off trouble like I have to tonight."

Dodd scowled, then shrugged and shifted straight. "Right."

Eli's gaze raked the cowboy. "That shirt'll stand out. Why not wear a dark one?"

Dodd gave a bitter smile. "A red shirt's always been my style. The color don't show blood." He opened the door. "I'm for a bite of supper. Want to come?"

Chapter 29

Morgan had lost his appetite about the time Eli Foster walked through his door. But his last meal had been breakfast, and he didn't know when he'd get the chance for food again. Trouble was the hotel dining room had filled with folks who'd waited for the storm to pass before getting out.

He headed for Jake's Place. Once he'd stepped out into the close, late afternoon air, he let his last assignment percolate through his mind. Destroy *The Wylder Sun*. Of course he wouldn't do it, but best not let Foster know just yet. Morgan couldn't expect action from one of his stops in Cheyenne this quick.

But how the devil could he postpone this? He hadn't thought the boss would act so quickly. More time… His thoughts stopped, and his body tensed.

Ray Horton swung onto the walk a half block ahead. Looked like he planned to eat at Jake's too. For once he was alone. Morgan's muscles eased a mite. He'd ignore the other gunman.

Fate was a conniving bitch. The only table left when he pushed through the café's door was next to Ray's. Morgan sat, avoiding eye contact, and gave his order. As the waitress poured coffee, Ray moved around his table to a chair closer to Morgan.

"Looks like tonight's gonna be some fun, huh?"

The odor of liquor on Ray's breath traveled all the

way to Morgan.

"Quiet. Do you want the whole place to know the boss's business?"

Ray chuckled, but his face took on a wary look. In a murmur, he taunted, "Bet your fine lady's gonna be right unhappy when she finds out who put her out of the gossip business."

Morgan bit the side of his lip to keep from answering. Ignoring the other man, he sipped his coffee.

"'Course, I could take that job off your hands if you'd rather visit your little girly in her bed. Or I could visit her for you, make sure she's occupied while you work."

"Shut up." Morgan stood, shoving his chair with the backs of his legs. "You don't talk that way about a lady. And stay away from her."

Ray's faded blue eyes squinted, the expression hardened. "Now, now, better calm down. Don't want the whole place knowing what you'll be up to later. 'Sides, I'm just pulling your leg. I got my assignment too."

As if she'd timed her return apurpose, the waitress wound her way around the other tables. Balancing the loaded tray on her hip, she set plates before each man, giving Morgan a speaking glare.

Pity he couldn't hear what that stare said.

He forced himself to clean his plate and finish his coffee. All without another word to Ray. But when Morgan rose to leave, the other man cut him a glance and gave a slow smirk.

Morgan hadn't had a chance to change when Foster showed up earlier, so he returned to his hotel room to don fresh trousers and to pack his gear. Then he stretched out on the bed. It wasn't long before the hot, thick air of the room forced him up to open the lone window a little. Winds had shifted direction and picked up power.

He gave a grim smile at the changeable weather. If the warm gusts continued, they'd go a long way to drying out what the rain had saturated. Lying down again, he closed his eyes. Might as well rest while he had the time.

When he awoke, the room was dark. Muffled shouts and curses, sounds of horses' hooves and creaking leather mingled with a faint tinkling of an out-of-tune piano from a tavern. The town had awakened as well. It was Friday night. A lot of cowhands and soldiers on leave would pile in for a night of rousing fun. Then Saturday night, a different group would take to the taverns—and streets.

Morgan splashed his face with lukewarm water from the pitcher, dragged damp fingers through his hair, then reached for his hat. After strapping on his gun belt, he checked his Peacemaker and unlocked the door.

Well on to ten o'clock, he saw when he reached the lobby. Good and dark. No moon to speak of. He ambled across the street, looking as if he headed to the sheriff's office. Slipping around the corner of the sheriff's office, Morgan continued his nonchalant stride to the *Sun.* Silently cursing the mud between buildings, he made it around back. No one to see him enter, that way.

He fished out his pocketknife and slid the blade into the opening between the door and frame. In less than a minute, he'd worked open the lock and was inside. Remembering where he'd seen a lamp hanging, he reached for a hook on the inside wall. There. He pulled a small metal box from his shirt pocket and took out a match.

When the lantern burned steadily, he turned down the wick as low as he could while still being able to make out objects. He only hoped Emily would understand what he was about to do.

****

Emily came awake instantly. *What?*

Silence. Then a rattle sounded, like a door handle jiggling. Was someone trying to break in? Convinced she'd been followed home a few times these past two weeks, although she'd seen a figure only twice, she'd had Tommy install inside locks to the front and back doors. Just last night, she'd watched from the back window, but the dark figure kept walking down the alley. As it always did. Still…

At a thump from the front porch, she threw back the sheet, eased from the bed, then crept into the parlor. Her eyes adjusted easily to the dark, and she made out a shadow at the front door. It moved to a side window, and a grate of wood on wood sounded as the sash slowly rose.

In the tiny house, the stove stood nearby, and she grabbed the poker. "Stop right there. I have a weapon." The sudden sound of her own voice nearly made her flinch.

Before she could advance and swing the piece of iron, the intruder stood before her.

"Now, now, pretty lady. I didn't come to hurt you. Why don't you put that thing down so's we can have us a talk?" The figure, dark against the faint illumination her eyes could differentiate, showed the invader was a man. The voice confirmed it. The voice—and her nose—also confirmed he'd been drinking.

"If you're not here to hurt me, what do you want?"

"Jest a little talk. You been causing some trouble hereabouts with them stories you're writing. Some of our townfolks don't like it. I reckon it's time for you to get on back to whatever fancy city you come from."

How dare someone threaten her over a story. "You can tell your townsmen that I print the truth. I'm not leaving, and no bully will make me."

As she spoke, she inched one foot forward, then the other, hoping her words distracted him. If she could get closer, she could swing—

"I'd stay put if I was you," came the voice. "Said I didn't *want* to hurt you. Don't mean I won't. If I'd wanted to hurt you, I could 'a come right in any of them nights I walked you home."

So this is who followed me. She paused. *Keep him talking while I think.* "What stories do you mean?"

"Women got no business pushing their noses into men's affairs."

"You mean men's affairs like politics and running people off their lands so it can be bought for cents on the dollar? I think you underestimate women, and men too."

"You mean that gunman outta Texas? The one's been sniffing at your skirts lately?" The voice in the dark took on a mean, hateful edge. "Wouldn't bet your last curl on that. Know where he is right now? Taking apart your precious newspaper."

"No." Emily stilled, stunned at his words. He lied. Morgan wouldn't do that. He did say he had one last job. But he knew how much the *Sun* meant to her.

Surely not. The identity of the intruder hit her. "You work for Eli Foster, don't you?"

"I sure do. Jest like him." The shadow lunged forward.

Instinctively, Emily brought the iron rod down, but the man ducked under the swing and grabbed her wrist. With his other hand, he latched on to the shoulder of her nightgown.

She kicked flat-footed, her heel thwacking his shin.

"Shit." He let go of her wrist and wrenched the poker from her numb fingers. At the same time, she jerked away. A loud rip tore through the darkness as the sleeve of her gown came loose. "Damn it."

He grabbed for her again, this time snagging the gown's neck. Emily scrambled away but tripped over a footstool and fell to one knee. The cotton fabric gave way again, and she felt a cool breeze bathe her neck and throat.

She scrambled to her feet and pushed the footstool toward her assailant. When he fell over it belly-first, a loud "Me-ow" sounded, and the intruder swore again. "Ow! Get away, cat." A dull thunk was followed by a pitiful "merow."

Emily scrambled to the back door and wrenched it open.

She ran.

Down the alleyway to the strip of land behind the buildings facing Wylder Street. Her bare feet connected with sharp rocks and slimy mud. A sharp jab to her heel made her wince, but she limped ahead.

Behind her the sound of pursuit rose over her thundering heartbeat and panting breath. If she could make it to the *Sun*, she could take cover.

But what if that man told the truth? What if Morgan was there? The sheriff's office sat just a few feet from the paper. She'd go there.

When she gained the back of her office, she saw a flicker of light. She stopped short. Over great gulps of air, she heard footsteps pounding closer. No time to circle the small building and try for the sheriff. The office it had to be.

She wrenched open the door and stumbled inside. Stopped at what she saw.

And all fight left her.

In the dim light of the oil lamp, Morgan worked methodically to wreck the place.

Metal letters were dumped from their racks. Back issues littered the floor. As she dragged her feet toward the front and around the shelter of the bookcase, tears filled her eyes. Her desk was on its side, the drawer upended.

A high, distraught "Ohhhh" wrenched from her throat.

Morgan froze from dismantling a small table, glanced up. "What are you doing here?"

Chapter 30

"Why?" Emily sobbed. "Why? I trusted you."

Morgan stared at her in disbelief. What in hell had brought her here tonight? How would he ever explain? Then she moved into the faint light, and his dismay turned to anger and fear—for her. He snatched the lamp with one hand, with the other he turned the flame as high as it would go. When he looked at her again, bile burned his throat.

She stood in her nightgown, one sleeve hanging from the wristband, the neckline gaping from a tear that exposed a bloody scratch across the top of one white breast. Her hair fell in clumps nearly to her waist, and her feet—good God, blood spotted her feet, what he could see beneath the mud. It squished between her toes, smeared around her ankles.

He held her as she trembled and wept. Panic molded his words into sharp angles. "Are you all right? What's happened?"

One after another, visions of different disasters shot through his mind. He wrapped her in arms, then tried to blot the thin blood streak on her chest. It looked like a fingernail gouge. "It's all right my darling, you're safe now."

She'd been attacked. He'd tear the bastard apart. He'd not let anything or anyone harm her, ever again.

At the sound of the back door slamming, he looked

up. Ray smirked at the edge of the lamplight. "Now ain't that sweet. I told you what he was up to, didn't I, pretty lady?"

Morgan brought Emily's chin up with his fingers. Voice hoarse and breaking, he asked, "Did this scum attack you?"

She sniffed and swiped her gown's intact arm across her nose. "Not like that. At least… I don't know why he came to my house."

"You should never open your door this late at night when you don't know who's knocking." He hadn't meant to sound scolding, but his concern made his tone rough.

She pulled away and turned. "I didn't open the door to him. I'm not a fool."

Suddenly, Morgan wanted to smile. She was all right. If his girl could snap off a retort that smartly, she wasn't seriously hurt. Then her words sank in. "If you didn't, then…"

"He broke through a window."

He raised his head to catch Ray's glare. "I was just explainin' to her that she oughta go back to the city and mind her own business. Let Wylder folks mind theirs. Of course, she needed to know what you were up to, all the time you was sweet-takin' her. Or did it go further than that?"

Morgan grasped Emily by the shoulders and set her to the side. When she took a breath, he murmured, "Hush." He looked into her eyes, and all his damned murky plans came clear. He loved her. Of course he did. And he'd be damned if he let her go.

He straightened and in a cold, dead voice, said, "You shouldn't have touched her."

"She came at me with a stove poker. What should I do, let her whack me? I was just protectin' myself."

"Protecting yourself against a lady in a nightgown who you just woke from a deep sleep. I can see how she might have been a danger to a man with a gun at his hip and a score to settle."

"Told you I had a job tonight too, didn't I?"

"You mean Foster set you after Miss Martin, to scare her into leaving?"

Ray snorted. "He must'a thought your heart wasn't in tearing up this place." He gave a slow look around. "Looks like he was wrong. Didn't I tell you, girly?"

Morgan's anger boiled up a notch with every word Ray uttered. Finally, he took a stance. Full height, loose arms.

"Oh, ho. You gonna challenge me now, big man? Gonna shoot me dead for daring to lay a finger on your woman?" He held out his hands to the side while he continued his taunt. "Don't reckon the sheriff will blink a kind eye to murder."

Morgan tuned out the mocking words as he struggled to get control of his temper. In all his years on the trail, he'd never faced another man like this. His work was always business, not personal feuds that led to showdowns. He'd like to put a bullet in Ray Horton's heart, but he didn't have the taste for cold-blooded killing. Not even now.

And not in front of the woman he loved. Even if she hated him for what he'd done to her precious business. He'd hoped to explain his plan in the morning when they met, before she saw it. Too late now. Wouldn't make a bit of difference to her.

Morgan smiled. He could see how irritated that

made Ray. He didn't give a damn. "No, Ray, I'm not going to shoot you, although you deserve it. Not only did you terrorize an innocent lady, I'm thinking back, wondering where you were on the night Sven Olsen was shot. None of the men saw you at the ranch. Bobby had some interesting stories to tell about you. And where you might be storing a little extra cash."

When Morgan began to talk, Ray looked a mite confused. But by the time he'd finished, Ray looked angry, defensive, and not a little scared.

"Emily, go get the sheriff. I'll bet he'd like to hear some of those stories."

Regardless of her appearance, Emily moved to the door. "I'll be right back."

He should have known enough not to take his eyes off Ray, but he did. He sent her a split-second look of approval. And in that instant, Ray went for his gun. Morgan knew by the way Emily's eyes widened, even before she called, "Look out."

He pulled his gun as he felt a hard, sharp jab to his upper back. He turned as he fell, and he shot. Just like he'd practiced all those years ago after the war.

As he'd once told Emily, he wasn't the fastest draw, but he was efficient, and deadly.

That one shot took Ray right between the eyes

Shock froze Emily with her hand on the door latch. She watched in horror as Morgan collapsed. Oh, dear heavens. Was he dead?

"No." The word wailed out as she ran to his side. He couldn't die. She loved him. She struggled to turn him over. Thank God, he still breathed. She was unbuttoning his shirt when the door burst open, and Sheriff Hanson dashed in.

"What's this?" he demanded, his gray moustache twitching as he looked from body to body.

"Get Doc Sullivan. Mr. Dodd's been shot."

Emily followed the sheriff's gaze to Ray, who lay unmoving. "He's dead. He shot" –she hiccupped— "Morgan in the back. But he's alive."

The youth who worked at the sheriff's office came straggling in, stubbing his toe at the doorway.

"Go get Doc," ordered the sheriff. When the boy left, Sheriff Hanson turned to Emily and untied a kerchief from around his neck. "Make this into a pad. See if we can stop the bleeding. Meanwhile, fill me in on what happened."

Fighting tears, Emily tried to summarize events of the past hour. But she kept forgetting points and backtracking. Until finally the sheriff held up a hand. "I think I got the idea, ma'am. Now before the whole town shows up to see what the commotion's all about, why don't you get a drink of water. And you might want to go home, put on some clothes."

His gruff voice and blunt words were softened by a quick grin. She nodded but turned her attention back to Morgan, who lay motionless. "Will he be all right, do you think?"

"I'm not a doctor, ma'am, but I've seen plenty of gunshots, and this 'un looks high enough. I expect he'll pull through." The door opened to admit the boy and Doc Sullivan. "Here's somebody who can say for sure."

After the doctor made a quick exam of Morgan, he ordered the boy to fetch a couple more men to carry the patient. "We'll take him to my office. Got to get that bullet out, but looks like he'll make it. If he don't lose more blood."

The sheriff helped Emily stand and that's when she got a good look at her gown. Sleeve torn off, neckline ripped down, front spattered with blood. And mud. She gasped and started for the back door. "I'll see you as soon as I'm decent, Doctor."

****

Morgan opened his eyes to the sun shining through a gaily checked yellow and white curtain. He lay in bed in a strange house, and his shoulder hurt like a stampede had trampled it. He turned his head to find Emily sitting in a chair. When she met his eyes, her lips came out from between her teeth, and her forehead uncrumpled.

"You're awake," she breathed. "Well, that was a silly thing to say. Of course you are. How do you feel?"

"I heard voices." Doc Sullivan poked his head around the corner of the door. "You just stay put. Miss Emily here will bring you some broth if you're hungry."

"I'd rather have some answers." Morgan hardly recognized the gravelly voice that came from his mouth.

It took most of the morning for him to hear all the details. Ray's death had been ruled self-defense. Eli Foster was horrified when he learned his foreman had done such a dastardly act as shoot his fellow Bar F employee in the back. And attack a lady! The man must have gone mad.

"He always was a jealous type," the sheriff said Eli told him. "But I feel sorry for him, and I'll see he's buried in the cemetery." He'd also assured the doc that he'd cover all the bills for Morgan. "A fine man. Loyal. He must have found out Ray had torn up the *Sun* before he tried to attack Miss Martin."

So that was the story Foster was going with. When the two men finally left, Emily remained. This was the first time they'd been alone since he regained consciousness. Tired or not, he had to have answers.

"First, tell me if that bastard hurt you in any way?" He took her hand.

She studied their entwined fingers. "Not in the way you mean. He frightened me at first, then he made me so angry I could have chewed nails, as my grandmother would say. I'm not physically harmed."

He didn't miss her use of "physically."

"Before you say anything else, let me explain," he started before she could draw another breath. "Foster gave me one last job before I quit. To wreck the *Sun* so you couldn't print anything more to interfere with his winning the election."

"Couldn't you have said no?" Her soft voice barely reached him.

"He, uh, said…that is…" Damn, how could he tell her the depths the man would have sunk to see his will carried out.

Emily squeezed his hand. "He threatened me, didn't he?"

"In a way. So I figured if I rearranged things to look like it had been torn apart, he'd be fooled. And we could set everything to rights quickly."

A small dimple appeared at the corner of her mouth.

"What?"

"I guessed as much. While you were sleeping this morning, I went through the office. The desk drawers were emptied into a box before they were overturned, the back issues were scattered in monthly groupings over the floor, even Charlie's type was arranged in order."

He rocked her hands gently. "And I was very careful not to scratch your freshly polished floor when I tipped your desk."

She laughed. "It was the most orderly chaos I've ever seen." She straightened and freed her hands. "There's some bad news, though. Doc says your wound will take a while to mend. You'll have to stay in Wylder for several more weeks. That means it might be too late to start for California before snow closes the passes."

Chapter 31

"About me leaving." Morgan recaptured her hands and tugged her closer. "Sit."

He lay silent for a bit after she perched on the bed. Then he said, "Our last night together was special. I think future nights could be even more special."

The bottom of her stomach hollowed. He was going to suggest an affair. She couldn't possibly—

"I told you once that after my job here, I'd planned to go—somewhere. The point was, I wasn't sure where, just a place to start over."

She nodded. "You mentioned California."

"I thought that for a long time. Then riding back from Laramie, I passed some nice ranches. Good land. It spoke to me."

He struggled, finally managing to sit. Hurt like hell, but that didn't matter. "I traveled rocks and canyons and space where you can see forever. On one side of me the mountains, on the other side, farms. Winters can be hard, I hear, and winds blow a mite. Most of the time." He stopped.

"What I'm trying to say is maybe I won't be riding on. I might like to settle here. And I wondered if you'd consider staying? It isn't what you're used to, no fancy social events, and the most important person you're likely to meet is the sheriff. That is, I can't offer you all the things you're used to, all the things you deserve."

Emily stared at her hands clenched in her lap. "Coming to Wylder, publishing the paper, has been a wonderful experience. But I always thought of it as a sort of vacation from my life in the city. Where I grew up, you know. But I've found I don't need fancy socials with people I don't know or have nothing in common with. Here—it's so different. People are wonderful and friendly, even when they're not."

Finally she looked into his eyes. "But also I'm not the kind of woman you must think I am. That is...after that night. I know I behaved like—"

"Shh." He cupped her cheek in his hand and brushed his thumb over her lips. "You know what kind of woman I think you are? Caring, giving, smart, capable. And damned beautiful.

"Nothing was wrong with that night except it had to end. You were wonderful. I should apologize for forgetting myself. I could have kissed you all night. But it had to stop, before you got hurt."

"Then...what?" she asked.

He was at a loss for words. He had no business asking anything of a lady like her, but God, he wanted to. Did he deserve a chance to change? When he went to church, back when he was young and life was full of hope, the preacher said God forgives if we're truly sorry for what we've done. Could He forgive a drifter, a gunhand?

Could Emily forgive, could she want someone so different from what she'd known?

He had to take the chance. No use prolonging his misery if she said no. "First, you should know I'm not wanted anywhere. Nobody's going to be looking for me to decorate a hanging tree."

She placed her hand over his mouth. "Shh." She got that secret little smile he loved. Then she said, "What's second?"

"My name's not Morgan Dodd."

At that she straightened and raised her eyebrows.

"I was christened Daniel Dodd Morgan. Dodd was my mother's maiden name. I changed it after the war. Didn't want any trails leading back to Missouri."

"Daniel Dodd Morgan. That's a wonderful name. The name of an esteemed, revered man."

He laughed then winced at the pain in his back. "Revered?"

She trailed her fingertips across his forehead. "Umm-hmmm."

"I can't give you a city life."

"Why would you worry about giving me any kind of life?"

He stilled. He wasn't any good at this. Probably making all kinds of a fool of himself.

She leaned forward, brushed his lips with hers. "You have to make yourself clear."

"Damn it, woman, I'm trying to ask you to marry me."

"Thank goodness you finally got to it." She gave him a brief smack. When she tried to rise, he held her for a real kiss. Finally she pulled back, gasping.

"So what's your answer?"

"Yes, of course. I love you. I think I have for a long time now but wouldn't admit it to myself. After all, we haven't spent months courting."

"Out here, time moves differently."

"I don't need all those things you think I do. I want friends, a happy home, a town where people care. If too much, sometimes."

She cuddled against his chest again, careful to lie on his uninjured side. He loved her for her consideration. For her consideration…also. But he had to tell her one last thing before the whole town knew.

"Third. Eli Foster is bound for prison." When she tried to sit up, he held her close. "That day in Cheyenne when I said I had to wrap up a couple of things? I met with a U.S. Marshal, turned over some information I'd gathered, along with a couple of documents from Bobby. The marshal's going to verify Foster's land purchases and look into his influence peddling as a railroad agent."

"So it's a matter of time, no matter how he rearranges his stories to make himself look good?" After another silence she said, "Isn't there a fourth?"

As if their minds aligned, he knew what she meant. He'd admitted it to himself not long ago.

"Fourth—and it should have been first—I love you, Emily Martin."

She sighed. "That's all I need. And I love you"— she kissed his cheek—"whatever your name is."

Epilogue

The next issue of *The Wylder Sun* carried a much-edited version of Ray Horton's death, but the report of Morgan Dodd's valiant rescue of the editor took on a poetic quality that won Morgan a few chuckles and hoots from men he knew.

That Friday's issue was to be the last before the mayor's election. And the last Emily handled alone.

Sunday's train brought the U.S. Marshal and three Union Pacific national officials. It also carried David Martin home to Wylder. He added what he'd gathered against Foster before the marshal, aided by Sheriff Hanson—"I wouldn't miss it for the world"—arrested Eli Foster on a variety of federal charges. Several county and territorial ones were added, just in case he managed to talk himself out of anything once he got back East.

Somehow, with the excitement of the arrest on Monday, the election never got around to being held. Horton insisted he was mighty relieved he could run the telegraph office in peace and quiet.

Three weeks later, Emily's family arrived from Missouri for a long visit—and the wedding, set for September 9.

Emily snuggled close in Morgan's arms the night before the ceremony. "My parents love you," she whispered, "especially Mother. You've worked your charm on her."

When he tried to claim he had no charm to work, she silenced him with another kiss. "Dad still says you should read the law, but he finally understands your heart is here. I think he had visions of your full name in gold letters on the door."

After a long, satisfying time, she sighed. "It's hard to call you Daniel," she admitted. "I suppose people will think it odd if I call my husband by his last name."

"Call me what you like," he whispered, nibbling her ear. "I have more news. I learned this afternoon that the bank accepted my bid on the Bar F. We'll call it the Double M. Think you'd be happy living that far from the newspaper?"

"I'm happy to turn over those worries to David. I'll contribute an article now and then." She sat up, the side of her lower lip grasped between her teeth. "Of course, I'll have to come to town for the Ladies' Committee on Voting."

He laughed and pulled her down beside him. "Of course you will. The unconventional Mrs. Morgan."

On the beautiful Sunday afternoon, Daniel Dodd Morgan and Emily Eloise Martin were wed in Wylder's St. Joseph's Episcopal Church. A reception was held afterward on the narrow lawn between the rectory and the Wylder School.

In a brief moment between congratulations from friends and ribbing from his new crew—Willie in the lead—Morgan turned away to drag in a breath. His gaze caught the line of white clouds crowning the western mountains. No longer did they beckon him, no longer did they promise a new beginning, a new life.

He had his new beginning. This life in Wylder was

the one for him. The past was gone. This was his future, here, with the woman he loved and their children to come.

Warmth surrounded his contented heart, and he turned back to the celebration.

A word about the author...

Multi-award-winning author Barbara Bettis can't recall a time she didn't love adventures of daring heroes and plucky heroines. A retired journalist and college English and journalism teacher, she lives in Missouri where she tries to keep her grandchildren supplied with cookies. When she's not editing for others, she's working on her own stories with heroines to die for-- and heroes to live for. http://www.barbarabettis.com